Sufficient Carbohydrate

Sufficient Carbohydrate

Dennis Potter

faber and faber

LONDON·BOSTON

First published in 1983
by Faber and Faber Limited
3 Queen Square London WC1N 3AU
Reprinted 1989
Filmset by Wilmaset Birkenhead
Printed in Great Britain by
Richard Clay Ltd Bungay Suffolk
All rights reserved

British Library Cataloguing in Publication Data

Potter, Dennis
Sufficient carbohydrate.
I. Title
822'.914   PR6066.01

ISBN 0-571-13261-8

For Jane, Sarah, Robert

CHARACTERS

JACK BARKER
EDDIE VOSPER
LUCY
CLAYTON
ELIZABETH

At the time of going to print the première of this play has been scheduled to open on 8 December 1983 at the Hampstead Theatre, Swiss Cottage Centre, London, in a production directed by Nancy Meckler and designed by Tanya McCallin.

The play takes place in the living room and terrace of a superior stone-built villa on a small, unspoilt Greek island to the west of the mainland.

The living room has a wide, open, stone stairway coming down into it from the landing and bedrooms above. The door into the kitchen is near the stair. The room opens out on to a stone terrace which looks down over a small olive grove to the sea: the sea is where the audience is. At one side of the terrace is a small section of low stone wall. There are steps off the terrace on to a path away from the villa, and there is another exit (on the same side) in the living room.

The villa has been rented by a multi-national food-processing company (parent company in Indiana) called Greenace Inc., and two of its senior executives are sharing a vacation.

They are JACK BARKER, a mid-forties Englishman demonstrably going to seed, and EDDIE VOSPER, a somewhat younger American, who is in fact Jack's superior in the company.

Eddie is accompanied by his second wife LUCY, a darkly beautiful American of about 30, and his 16-year-old son by his first marriage, CLAYTON, a youth who scarcely knows his father and has been invited along from Indianapolis to make up the party.

Jack is with his wife ELIZABETH, in her mid-thirties, and very attractive in a cool English manner.

EDDIE and JACK work for Greenace in Norfolk, England, at an old British food company that has been taken over by Greenace.

The play takes place on a Saturday (Act One) and Sunday (Act Two) at the end of the first week of the holiday.

There is an interval between the acts.

ACT ONE

SCENE ONE

It is not yet six o'clock in the morning. The light grows from near-dark to soft grey, allowing the audience to distinguish first the silhouette and then the distinct details of JACK BARKER.

He has slept badly, and he came down to the stone terrace fronting the elegantly spacious living room of the villa an hour or so before, to await the dawn. JACK's *hair is tousled, and he is still in his striped pyjamas— which he would insist on wearing in bed even on the Equator itself, let alone this Greek island. He is sitting on the little stone wall at the side of the terrace, looking rather miserably out to sea, and sipping what looks like orange juice.*

Silence. Then JACK *speaks, in a monotone, and apparently to no one, with total desolation.*

JACK: No. You're not there. You're not there, are you? You never were there, were you? No. Definitely not. No. Never. Never. (*Fractional pause.*) Why not? Why aren't you? Boring old bugger!
(*Then he hears the cistern flush somewhere behind and above him. Someone in the villa is on the move.* JACK *does not look around.*)
Good morning good morning good morning. How nice how very nice to see you dear. How—nice. The sun is not up yet, so why are you?
(*On to the open stairway into the living room comes awkwardly gangling 16-year-old* CLAYTON VOSPER, *dressed ready for an early swim, and carrying a book. When he sees* JACK *he half breaks his cheerful stride, clearly very wary of the Englishman.* JACK *turns. It seems he expected someone else. There is a persistent hint of mockery, even aggression, in his voice.*)
Oh. Good morrow, Clayton, old chap. My goodness, you are an early riser.

CLAYTON: Hi, Jack. Yeh. What time is it?

JACK: Tick tock. Nearly six o'clock and all's almost well. The best part of the day. It's not so bloody hot.

CLAYTON: That's right.

JACK: But any moment now the sun will burn a hole in the sky. And the bloody cicadas will start rubbing their bloody legs against their bodies. It's a bloody complicated form of masturbation, don't you think?

CLAYTON: I—ah—I don't hear them any more. The first two days they really get to you—but they don't bother me now.

JACK: Yes. I find it's the same with people. Don't you agree? Of course you do.

(CLAYTON *looks cautious.*)

CLAYTON: Some people. Maybe.

JACK: Very fair-minded, aren't you?

CLAYTON: What?

JACK: When you get older, Clayton, you'll think you are getting wiser. But you only get shabbier. Believe me.

CLAYTON: Oh, come on.

JACK: No, no. Take me, for example. Insomniac, because I've nothing whatsoever to dream about. How's about that, then? Don't you think that's sad, young man?

(CLAYTON *does not want this—and* JACK *knows it.*)

CLAYTON: Is there any juice left—?

JACK: Oh, there might be a trace here and there. But very little of it actually reaches my loins—

CLAYTON: No, sir. I meant orange juice—!

JACK: So you did. So you did. No. I drank it all. Sorry.

(*He finishes the juice, then looks, oddly challengingly, at* CLAYTON.)

CLAYTON: That's OK.

JACK: The buxom little maid will no doubt bring gallons more this morning. I was too hot to sleep—and very thirsty. There wasn't much else to drink. I don't want to start on the Scotch at (*Half sings*) four o'clock in the morning.

CLAYTON: Is that when you came down?

JACK: It was, indeed. All the way down.

(CLAYTON *obviously wants to get away, and moves to do so.*)

CLAYTON: Well, I guess I—

JACK: The elegant Mrs Barker, my dear wife, *snores*, would you believe. And so does your father, by the way. I can hear him rattling the rafters at the other end of the villa.

CLAYTON: Maybe he's trying to scare the mosquitoes.

(*He laughs, then stops, awkwardly adolescent, when* JACK *doesn't.*)

JACK: Those two ought to share the same bedroom, my wife, your father. Let snore cleave unto snore, eh?

(CLAYTON *doesn't answer.* JACK *looks at him, nastily amused.*)

I said they should sleep in the same room. Don't you think that's a good idea, Clayton? I mean—hasn't it ever crossed your mind that such an arrangement would make a lot of sense?

CLAYTON: Um. No—

JACK: Do you mean No, it isn't a good idea, or No, you haven't considered it? Mind you, your stepmother would undoubtedly object, judging by the way she—

CLAYTON: (*Interrupting*) What are you talking about?

(JACK *looks at him, then turns away abruptly.*)

JACK: Did you see the ship pass?

CLAYTON: What ship?

JACK: Every morning at about half-past five an old black freighter trundles across the horizon over there.

CLAYTON: No. I didn't catch it—

JACK: I wasn't up on our first morning here, but I've seen it on the last four mornings. It must be the cargo boat which tramps across from Brindisi and puts in to the Greek mainland at about seven o'clock. It reminds me of my own childhood because it brings back all the sea stories I used to read as a boy marooned in a country vicarage. Ahoy, there! Et cetera. Trouble is, it reminds me of something else, too. Something delicious or terrible or—which I've either forgotten, or haven't yet had. Something gone for ever or awaiting me for ever.

CLAYTON: I know the feeling—

JACK: Do you? Do you really?

CLAYTON: Well—it's—kind of like . . .

(*But* JACK, *full of vague, unhappy yearning—and scarcely suppressed hostility—is not really interested in a reply. He turns away again, abrupt, looking out to sea.* LUCY VOSPER *appears on the stairs during* JACK'*s next speech. She seems to decide to hang back, not yet noticed. She listens.*)

JACK: When it passes, the ship, the light is even more opaque than it is now. Sort of—marbled. And cool. There are a few wisps of mist curling about an inch from the top of the sea, and yet the water is still that impossible blue—It's all like when the world began, and God Saw That It Was Good— (*Bitter little laugh.*) A chalice full of the warm South. The sea, slap–slapping itself. The little olive trees catching hold of the rocks. Space. Air. And an uncertain smudge which sort of—*solidifies* out of the ache in the mind and very slowly becomes a black freighter dragging itself across the edge of the world—For a moment—a whole minute—it's all so perfect you want to reach out and—and pull it into your soul. You want to pick it all up—and *eat it.* (*He turns.*) Do you understand?
(*There is, now, an intensity in the question which troubles the boy, who responds with a strained laugh—the kind that is bound to leave him stranded when* JACK *does not respond.*)

CLAYTON: That would be one heck of a mouthful.
(JACK *stares at him.* CLAYTON *wilts.* LUCY, *still unseen, goes to speak. Then—*)

JACK: That's not junk food out there, laddie. Not the kind of predigested pap Greenace vomits out into the supermarkets.

LUCY: Bad-mouthing the company again, are we, Jack?

JACK: There aren't any hidden mikes here, are there, Lucy?

LUCY: I hope so. But what are we all doing up so early—?

CLAYTON: I'm going for a swim.

LUCY: You want me to fix coffee or something?

CLAYTON: No—it's OK—OK. I'll have it when I come back. I'll—bye—
(*And he lopes off, awkwardly.* JACK *looks at* LUCY, *maliciously amused.*)

JACK: He can't wait to get away. Can he?

LUCY: But from what?

JACK: You look—terrific. It must be disturbing for a boy of that age to have a stepmother as beautiful as you.

LUCY: As long as it doesn't disturb *you.*

JACK: Me? Oh, everything disturbs me, sweetie.

13

LUCY: Yes. Obviously.

(*She says it so crisply he is surprised.*)

JACK: What do you mean—obviously? I think you should be a bit more tentative. It becomes you more. (*Sniff.*) More or less.

LUCY: You weren't very nice to Clayton.

JACK: No?

LUCY: No.

(*Fractional pause. He seems to measure her, then drops his eyes.*)

JACK: No. I suppose not—

LUCY: This vacation is going to be difficult for him—

JACK: For all of us, darling stepmother.

LUCY: (*Ignoring this*) He finds it hard to relate to his father, and he doesn't know me—not yet. Don't forget he lives with his mother back in Indiana. This is his first trip outside the States.

JACK: I feel it's mine, too!

LUCY: What?

JACK: This tiny island has no Coca Cola signs, no muzak, no hamburgers, not a sniff of cocaine or a single sud of a sodding soap opera, no muggers, nothing—no amenities whatsobloodyever. It's as though America lived in vain. Everywhere else I've been—especially ye olde England—is a pocket-sized imitation of the Land of the Free—

LUCY: Thank God.

JACK: Oh, come now. There's no need to be blasphemous.

LUCY: Is that British sarcasm? Or just plain old British snobbery?

JACK: No. It's me. Just me. Bilious old me. Don't worry—

LUCY: Oh, but I'm not. You don't worry me at all, Jack.

JACK: —I know which side my homogenized, processed, New and Improved monosodium-glutamated food additive is buttered on. Greenace Incorporated pays my ample salary and arranges this adequate holiday—So what do I care if your countrymen leave their litter all over this planet and even on the far side of the sil–ver–y moon? I simply say to myself Pardon me, boy, is this the Chattanooga Choo Choo and sit back with my arse in clover and my head as empty

14

as Donald Duck on one of his better days. Quack.
Quack. Quack.
(*Tiny pause.*)

LUCY: Jack.

JACK: Yes, my sweet?
(*She hesitates.*)

LUCY: It doesn't matter—
(*He is instantly alert, even tense.*)

JACK: No, come on, Lucy. What were you going to say?

LUCY: I—it's not really my place to say it . . .

JACK: To say *what*? I'm all agog.

LUCY: (*Hesitant*) Well—have you thought—I mean, do you ever
wonder *why* Greenace should pay for this little jaunt—?

JACK: Oh, *esprit de corps*, I should think. Corporate glad-handing
for the chaps. What else?
(*But he is looking at her sharply.*)

LUCY: Maybe I should keep my big mouth shut, but if I were you—

EDDIE: (*On stair*) That's right, Lucy. Shut!
(*JACK looks from one to the other.*)

JACK: Hey—what *is* this?

EDDIE: *Good* morning, both. What is what, Jack? Is someone
making coffee?

LUCY: (*Quickly*) I'm just about to, Eddie.

JACK: No—wait a minute—what were you trying to tell me—?
Something for what *you*'d call My Own Good by the sound
of it. I'm fascinated. No—even better: I'm actually even
rather interested.
(*She darts a quick look at EDDIE, clearly flustered.*)

LUCY: Oh, I always get it wrong anyway—

EDDIE: (*Laugh.*) Put that in writing! Immediately!
(*Despite the laugh, EDDIE's annoyance is obvious. JACK's languid
affectation has instantly shifted to an alternate British mode: raging
paranoia.*)

JACK: Now look here—what have you got to keep quiet about,
Lucy? If it's something that affects me I ought to know
about it. Even if it's For My Own Good.

EDDIE: Aw, now, Jack—she's not Miss Lonelyhearts—

JACK: Aw, now, nothing! What's going on here?

(LUCY *is backing out.*)

LUCY: I'll make the coffee—Don't take me so seriously, Jack. Please.

JACK: (*To* EDDIE) What's all this about Greenace and if I were me, which, alas, I am. Some of the time.

EDDIE: And why shouldn't you be? Stay as bright as you are.

JACK: Come on, Eddie. Let's have it.

EDDIE: It's nothing to get steamed up about, Jack. I guess there are some people at Greenace who don't exactly want to fall down and kiss your feet about the way you sound off about things sometimes. But you know that, anyway.

JACK: Know it, and love it. Fortunately, I've my shares to keep me warm. (*Suddenly*) What things? Eddie—?

EDDIE: Christ, it's too early in the morning. Give me time to unpack the bags under my eyes.

JACK: You mean—my little jokes and what-have-you are getting up someone's nose—is that it?

EDDIE: (*Grimly amused*) You *could* say that.

JACK: Is it my drinking—? Do they mistake literacy for drunken incoherence? That's it, isn't it?

EDDIE: Hell, no! What's a hiccup or two in the boardroom.

JACK: Ah. So Greenace think I need a holiday—is that so they can turn my grandfather's portrait to the wall? A movement that would at least simulate the way he is undoubtedly turning in his grave—

EDDIE: (*Cutting in*) They think we both need some time away, Jack. That's all. So—let's enjoy. It's on the house.

JACK: Together. But why together? Eddie? We're not exactly buddy-boys, are we?

(ELIZABETH BARKER *is now coming down the stairs—to* EDDIE'*s relief.* EDDIE *instantly goes to greet her.* JACK *watches him, with a sudden added hostility.*)

EDDIE: Elizabeth. As immaculate at the dawn as at midnight! How do you do it?

ELIZABETH: Good morning, Eddie. What's the matter with you?

EDDIE: Ah. So cool. So crisp.

ELIZABETH: No. Rather damp and frayed, actually. (*Looks at her husband.*) Hello, hello. Got the black dog on our shoulders, have we?

(EDDIE *puts his finger to his lips, mock conspiratorial.*)

EDDIE: Late to bed and early to rise.

JACK: Be careful what you say, Elizabeth, and how you say it. We, the Barkers, are under observation. Or, at least, *I* am. There's probably a microphone under the lid of the loo. You know I never lift the seat.

ELIZABETH: What do you mean?

EDDIE: (*Laugh.*) Now, Jack—there are no buggers here. Except silly ones.

JACK: It seems this is no innocent holiday so generously provided by my beloved employer, dear—

EDDIE: Jack. Don't be ridiculous—

JACK: —but a kind of *test* or something to examine either my loyalty or my suitability or both. A sort of commercial McCarthyism. Just because I pee on the seat. (*Sniff.*) And a few other places.

ELIZABETH: Are you serious?

EDDIE: Of course not! Are you, Jack?

JACK: Then what was Lucy trying to tell me? Before you stopped her. Something For My Own Good. Who the fuck do you think you are, Eddie? Mrs Thatcher? Come on. What is it you want to say?

EDDIE: Only that you are sometimes a pain in the ass. Like right now.

ELIZABETH: Hear, hear.

JACK: Oh, thank you, Elizabeth. Very wifely of you. Thanks very much.

ELIZABETH: What's he on about, Eddie?

(LUCY *comes back in with coffee.*)

LUCY: My fault! Jack was sounding off about everything and nothing and I—(*Laugh.*)—oh, I'm sorry, Jack—I kind of hinted at dark and mysterious wheels within wheels just to tickle his paranoia for him. Coffee. Let's have coffee.

JACK: There always are wheels within wheels, Lucy. And it didn't feel as though you were *tickling*, my love.

EDDIE: Where's the juice? Bring me my juice!

LUCY: It's all gone.

17

EDDIE: No!

JACK: I was hot and thirsty. There wasn't much else to drink.

ELIZABETH: I thought you didn't like juice?

LUCY: That's right. You said it was an unhealthy American habit.

JACK: I—ah—I mixed it with a little gin. An unhealthy British habit.

ELIZABETH: In the *morning*, Jack?

LUCY: I noticed the empty Gordon's in the kitchen. Oops! I shouldn't have said that.

(*They look at him: tiny pause.*)

JACK: I spilt some.

ELIZABETH: Jack. What are you doing in your pyjamas?

JACK: What am I doing in my pyjamas? Quietly decaying, that's what. What do you think I'm doing?

LUCY: You don't wear them in bed, do you?

ELIZABETH: You bet he does! And with all the buttons done up.

EDDIE: What—on these hot nights—?

ELIZABETH: Poor Jack is the sort of Englishman who always wears a striped tie by day and striped pyjamas by night. Even if he was on the Equator itself.

(*As they laugh—*)

JACK: Poor Jack. What's this Poor Jack business? Is this to be my new status? That, and sentences beginning 'If I were you—'

ELIZABETH: There's nothing *new* about it, darling.

JACK: Can I tell you something, my love—

LUCY: Stea–dy!

JACK: I am sick and tired of the way you talk to me. It's as though I'm some snotty-nosed little schoolboy at the back of the class who hasn't turned in his homework on time. Well—I *haven't*—and I'm not going to!

ELIZABETH: You can't. You've spilt gin all over it.

JACK: Poor Jack is not going to play your miserable little games, thank you very much. Christ, you all address me as though I'm—

(ELIZABETH *piano-fingers her hand over her mouth in an exaggerated yawn.*)

18

ELIZABETH: Ho hum.

> (JACK *stares at her, his face twitching.* EDDIE *and* LUCY *look at each other*.)

JACK: (*Evenly*) Why are you such a cow, Elizabeth?

ELIZABETH: Why do you think?

JACK: I can't even begin to imagine. But you make me want to throw up. You're so fucking smug, I just—

EDDIE: Hey, fella—

> (*But* ELIZABETH *throws her head back and laughs, mockingly.* JACK *glares at her, then stalks away, up the stairs, rigid, wordless*.)

ELIZABETH: (*Calls after* JACK) And make sure you wash under your arms! Do you hear!

> (JACK *does not turn, or break step.* ELIZABETH *looks at the other two*.)

LUCY: Elizabeth—

ELIZABETH: (*Quickly*) Oh, God. I'm sorry. We're spoiling the holiday, aren't we?

EDDIE: Well—I wouldn't push him too far. . . . He hasn't got both his paddles in the water.

ELIZABETH: I was pretty disgusting, wasn't I?

LUCY: Yes. You were.

> (*Little pause.* ELIZABETH *sips coffee, thoughtfully*.)

ELIZABETH: Will you be honest with me, Eddie—

EDDIE: That depends, honey.

ELIZABETH: On what?

EDDIE: (*Parody*) On the percentages, baby.

ELIZABETH: Jack was on to something, wasn't he? About this holiday, I mean. They'd like to get rid of him, wouldn't they?

EDDIE: Well, now—let me switch off the tapes.

LUCY: (*Firmly*) No. Tell her.

> (EDDIE *hesitates, lowers his voice*.)

EDDIE: Jack hasn't been too happy with Greenace for some time—He can't or won't forget that it's no longer a little family company, *his* family company.

ELIZABETH: Oh, but that's only his *style*, surely.

EDDIE: I know all about his style. Christ, don't I just. He thinks every single one of his colleagues is either a moron or a philistine—and he's not very crazy about Americans, is he? Although he was happy enough to sign the take-over deal and pocket the cash.

ELIZABETH: He breaks the rules. That's supposed to be a secret English conspiracy.

LUCY: How do you mean?

ELIZABETH: Whenever two or three Englishmen are gathered together they will sooner or later start to wink and nudge and snigger about crude, vulgar, filthy rich and disgusting loud-mouthed Americans. We still can't help thinking of you as unreformed colonials just one step away from the spittoon. And England as the Greece to your Roman Empire—*civilizing* you.

EDDIE: That's Jack, all right. The Aristotle of the food-processing business. Plato among the pizzas.

ELIZABETH: But of course we don't *really* believe it. Not even Jack.

LUCY: (*Laugh.*) Don't be so sure!

ELIZABETH: No, no. He doesn't. It's just that he's going to seed even faster than dear old England is itself. I think he knows the game's up for him and his sort—

EDDIE: That's not true, Elizabeth. I hope very, very much that'll never be so. Every meat pie needs a bit of gristle.
(*Tiny pause.*)

ELIZABETH: You think I'm being horribly disloyal, don't you? No. Don't answer that. I know you do. And I *am*, in a way—

EDDIE: Look, every marriage has its own secret life, and it's not for us to—You sure go out of your way to skin the guy, I'll give you that.

ELIZABETH: But he wasn't just being paranoid. Was he?

EDDIE: Look—I'll tell you this—he's not doing his job, and they do want to get rid of him. But Jack's no fool. He's still got some of the original shares *and* a cast-iron contract. They'd like to make him an offer he can't refuse.

ELIZABETH: Who's they?

EDDIE: He's obstructing every decision ever made, all across the board. It'd almost be better if he stayed out longer for lunch than he already does. Say, till five instead of four.

ELIZABETH: And where do *you* stand on all this?

EDDIE: Elizabeth—I don't have as much clout as you think—

ELIZABETH: Are you saying you want him out, too?

LUCY: (*Too quickly*) Of course he isn't.

ELIZABETH: *Are* you, Eddie?

EDDIE: No. But—listen. I arranged this vacation so that we could—so that I could get through to him. Lay it out. Hell, *I* don't want him eased out. But there's more than one person knocking on his door.

ELIZABETH: Don't tell him that!

LUCY: But surely—

ELIZABETH: He'll never open it if he hears somebody breathing hard on the other side. He'll just hide under the desk, I promise you. He won't even answer the front door at home.

EDDIE: Why not?

ELIZABETH: In case it's a Jehovah's Witness.

(*They start to laugh.*)

LUCY He could get lucky. It might be a Mormon.

(*They laugh.* JACK *reappears on the stair, and looks down at them, sourly.*)

JACK: Having fun, are we?

(*They stop laughing, almost guiltily.*)

ELIZABETH: Yes, Jack. We are.

JACK: Jolly good. Keep it up.

EDDIE: Jack—do you want us to stand at attention, or what?

(JACK *joins them at the table, rather morose.*)

JACK: Hasn't the maid arrived yet?

LUCY: Not for another half hour.

ELIZABETH: Do you want breakfast?

(JACK *looks at her.*)

JACK: I want to eat something. But I don't think it's food.

LUCY: I think I'll join Clayton.

EDDIE: (*Surprised*) Is he up, then?

LUCY: He's gone swimming.

JACK: I think I scared him away. I'd forgotten exactly what is the sweet dread of adolescent youth.

EDDIE: What's that?

21

JACK: Conversation.

EDDIE: Yeh. I guess you're right at that.

(*A slightly awkward little pause.* LUCY *hesitates before leaving, perhaps sensing that something is going to happen.*)

ELIZABETH: You want some coffee, Jack?

JACK: No.

ELIZABETH: Oh, Jack! Please don't pull that sort of face.

JACK: What sort of face is that?

ELIZABETH: You've got a mouth like a pussy cat's bottom.

(EDDIE *laughs.* JACK *looks at him balefully.*)

JACK: It's about mushrooms, isn't it? This has something to do with the bloody mushrooms.

EDDIE: That's—ah—that's something we need to discuss at some point, sure. That, and related matters.

JACK: I thought so!

ELIZABETH: What on earth are you talking about—*mushrooms*?

LUCY: I'm off!

EDDIE: (*As she goes*) I'll be with you in a minute. Keep the water warm.

JACK: No you don't, Eddie. The sooner we get this thing settled the better.

ELIZABETH: You're not going to talk about *work*, are you? I thought this was supposed to be a holiday.

JACK: So did I, Liz. But we both thought wrong. (*At* EDDIE) Didn't we?

EDDIE: Jesus Christ on a bike.

JACK: No—come on! It's because I've been putting the research money into machines, isn't it? And you've been doing your damnedest to push it elsewhere, haven't you? We've been on entirely different paths, you and me, and you're trying to put the roadblocks up in front of me.

EDDIE: (*Wearily*) This is the wrong time, Jack—

JACK: Like hell it is! Well, I'm telling you! I know about the devious way you've gone back to head office in Indiafuck-inganapolis without any reference to me whatsoever—

EDDIE: I don't have to refer to you, Jack.

JACK: So you admit it!

EDDIE: When are you going to come to terms with reality, Jack?

Why don't you stop and think for *one minute* about the why and the where and the how of the way things get done at Greenace. Instead of pawing the ground all the time like some crazy bull? OK. Take your mushrooms. Have you bothered to find out—*ever*—what proportion of our total sales come from mushrooms—have you?

JACK: That's got nothing to do with it, and you—

EDDIE: Zero point nine eight. Less than one per cent, for Christ's sakes!

JACK: I'm talking about a general principle here, not bloody decimals.

EDDIE: (*Cutting in*) And do you know what proportion of the R and D budget you've already committed to this no-good harvester to pick the goddamn fungi? Nearly eight per cent! Now, that must be crazy in anyone's book. Can't you see that?

JACK: My God. You're so thick, I can't believe it. You just won't get hold of the fact that a variable harvester of the kind we need for mushrooms could be applicable to any other sort of crop that was not standard size.

EDDIE: The solution is not mechanical. It's biological. Every crop can be made standard size.

JACK: Bollocks!

EDDIE: The mushroom just so happens to be sexually unstable, and so if—

(*But* ELIZABETH, *who has been listening with apparent boredom, bursts out laughing.* EDDIE, *about to be irritated, instead grins and spreads his hands in rueful concession.* JACK, *agitated, is not a bit amused.*)

JACK: And if you or anyone else think that you can change the genetic code at less research cost than—Elizabeth! This is serious—!

ELIZABETH: (*Gurgle*) I'm sorry. But it can't be!

EDDIE: You're right, Elizabeth. We should let all fungi have some privacy at this time of the morning. I'm not feeling too sexually stable myself at the moment.

ELIZABETH: Ditto. Or likewise, as *you* say.

JACK: I'd appreciate it if you two would stop flirting with each other, and let me make the point—

ELIZABETH: Jack. Don't be such a *pain*, there's a darling.

JACK: Christ, Liz! Keep out of it! Keep your bloody nose out of it!

EDDIE: For Pete's sake, this is no way to talk things through. Why d'you get so hot under the collar?
(*But* JACK *hammers his fist into the palm of his hand, utterly enraged.*)

JACK: A mushroom is a mushroom is a fucking mushroom! They don't and they *won't* come in standard sizes—right? Not *real* mushrooms—*proper* mushrooms—they happen to reproduce in varying sizes because of their genetics—

EDDIE: Now hold on. Hold it right there—Jack—

JACK: But you and your lot want to change all that. Nature's not bloody good enough for you. It's all bloody biotech and microbes and membrane filtration and protein separation and—

EDDIE: Jack—!

JACK: —and—and—bacteria-fed methanol and—Jesus save us—fungal food in meat pies grown on waste nutrients. Well, this is where I make my stand! My grandfather's company used to put proper food on the shelves before fucking Greenace bought us out—and that's where our future lies. Quality! Who wants to eat out of a fucking test-tube! Give people like you their head and we'll all end up eating shit—literally, I mean. *Really* eating it!

EDDIE: Now you're being ridiculous.

JACK: Mind you, at least shit tastes of *something*—You know what they're working on now, Liz? A solution to dip fruit into, and so keep it on the shelves a few days longer. Sucrose esters of fatty acids and a polysaccharide! To block the fucking pores of the poor fucking banana!

ELIZABETH: Please don't shout.

JACK: They're so delighted with it, these morons! Why? Because it's odourless and tasteless and you can't even fucking *see* it! Just dunk in the fruit and stop it ripening. How about that! Eh? Eh? Shit might be better, at that!

EDDIE: Have you finished?

JACK: Finished, yes—I've finished! I've had it up to my jugular with you and Greenace and your devious methods. Don't think I don't know you're trying to push me out—well—don't bother, mate. Don't fucking bother! I know where the door is, and there's cleaner air outside! So count me out—d'you hear? Count me out! Shove your polysaccharide up your own filtered membrane!

(*Almost beside himself with impotent rage,* JACK *stalks away, virtually brandishing his fist.* EDDIE *and* ELIZABETH *look at each other. A moment.*)

EDDIE: I suppose, technically, that constitutes a resignation.

ELIZABETH: But Eddie—no—he wasn't being himself—

EDDIE: Oh, yes he was. That was Jack being very much himself. A rerun of what's been going on back in Norfolk. He gets so mad he goes up and down the corridors kicking the radiators.

ELIZABETH: (*Sigh*) Dear God.

(*They look at each other. There seems to be a current between them.*)

EDDIE: (*Quietly*) He's no fool, you know.

(*She stares at him, then shakes her head.*)

ELIZABETH: No. He doesn't know.

EDDIE: Don't be so sure. You think all *that* was about adulterated foodstuffs?

ELIZABETH: He hasn't the faintest idea.

(*Pause. He touches her face.*)

EDDIE: Maybe he's gone to throw himself off the rocks.

ELIZABETH: Of course not. He's almost certainly abusing the olive trees. And then he'll shake his fist at the bloody sun.

(*Pause.*)

EDDIE: Elizabeth.

(*She puts a finger to his lips.*)

ELIZABETH: No. Not here. No. Don't be silly.

(*Pause. Then they kiss, suddenly, and with hunger. Before they break,* CLAYTON, *in bare feet, and just his swimming trunks, comes back in. He watches, blankly. Then, unseen by them, backs out.*)

(*Breaking*) No, Eddie. We mustn't. We simply—must—not.

EDDIE: It was all that talk of membrane filtration and protein separation, Liz. Not to mention dipping bananas.

25

(*She puts her hand to his genitals.*)

ELIZABETH: Now, now. Don't be dirty.

SCENE TWO

The late evening of the same day—Saturday.

The sun has gone down. The dinner has been eaten. There are lights on in the living room, but out on the terrace there is some sense of the velvety darkness now surrounding the villa. All five are now out on this terrace in the various postures of postprandial relaxation, satiated and surfeited. Soon, the insects will drive them 'inside'. They are drinking wine—freely.

EDDIE: This is the best time of the day. (*Drinks wine.*) Easily the best. When the sun has gone down and the dinner is being digested. That was some meal. A Saturday night special!

JACK: (*Laconic*) Bang bang.

EDDIE: Cigar, Jack?

JACK: No thanks. Putting one of those in my mouth always makes me feel vaguely homosexual.

ELIZABETH: (*With an air of discovery*) Ah.

JACK: What do you mean—Ah?

ELIZABETH: What one usually means when one says Ah. *Ah*—so that's it! Or *Ah*—isn't that int–er–esting.
(*Comical little pause.*)

JACK: Yes, Eddie. Thank you. I *will* have a cigar.
(*They laugh.*)
(*Dreadful American accent*) I'm the Sheriff. And this is *my* town.

EDDIE: Sure. A cigar is a cigar is a cigar.
(*As* JACK *lights up*—)

LUCY: My back is peeling—and it aches. Like I was lying in nettles.

ELIZABETH: It was a real scorcher, wasn't it? (*Drinks wine.*) I think I lay too long in it myself. My brains feel as though they've been fried.

JACK: Ah!
· (*They laugh.*)

EDDIE: How did they do it in this heat? Those old Greeks.

LUCY: How did they do what? Smoke cigars?

EDDIE: No. Philosophize. Think consecutive thoughts—Hell!
   (*The* 'Hell!' *because something stings his forearm. He slaps at it.*)

ELIZABETH: You've got sweet blood, Eddie. They'll keep on
   biting. Some are sweet and some are salty. They don't
   touch Jack.

LUCY: (*Slight edge*) Do they bite you, Elizabeth?
   (ELIZABETH *looks at her. They briefly hold a challenging glance,*
   which EDDIE *notices.*)

EDDIE: Imagine squatting down on some hot rock or other and
   working out Transcendence or a new theory of Justice with
   goddamn insects biting your arm and the sweat trickling
   into your eyeballs. And not just your eyeballs, come to
   think of it.
   (*Pause.* ELIZABETH *yawns.* JACK *looks at* LUCY. CLAYTON *is*
   looking intently at LUCY. *She sees.*)

LUCY: You're very quiet, Clayton.

CLAYTON: Um. Yeh—

EDDIE: Everything OK, son? Enjoying yourself?

CLAYTON: (*Flat*) Sure. Great.

LUCY: What's that book you've been reading?
   (*He twitches, and shifts uncomfortably.*)

CLAYTON: Oh. Just—some stuff—

ELIZABETH: I tried to read this afternoon. When I was
   sunbathing. Stupid, really. I gave up when I had read the
   same line five times.

JACK: Did you understand it?

ELIZABETH: What?

JACK: The line. When you had read it five times.
   (CLAYTON *snorts in sudden amusement. Then is embarrassed.*)

CLAYTON: Sorry.

JACK: That's all right, old son. Don't apologize, for Christ's sake.
   I'm grateful for a little appreciation. (*Pours some more wine,*
   with an indulgent simper) And a little more lubrication.

ELIZABETH: Go easy, Jack.

JACK: What for?

ELIZABETH: Because you'll probably fall over when you stand

27

up. You've already finished off a whole bottle on your own.
(JACK *mockingly raises his glass to her.*)

JACK: O for a beaker full of the warm South,
   Full of the true, the blushful Hippocrene,

ELIZABETH: You're slurring your words.

JACK: —With beaded bubbles winking at the brim
      And purple-stainéd mouth;
    That I might drink, and leave the world unseen,
      And with thee fade away into the forest dim:

ELIZABETH: You're still slurring your words.

EDDIE: Yeh—and probably misquoting them, too.

JACK: What do you mean, misquoting?

EDDIE: Who's the blushful whatsit? Where's it from?

JACK: Where do you think? The *Reader's Digest*?
   (EDDIE *stares at him. Then—*)

EDDIE: I know it's Shakespeare. I don't know which play, that's all.
   (*Tiny pause. Then* JACK *throws back his head in a deliberately horrible, silent, open-mouthed parody of a laugh.*)

CLAYTON: (*Embarrassed*) It's Keats, Dad.
   (*Tiny pause.* ELIZABETH *and* LUCY *start to laugh.* EDDIE *appears completely unfazed.*)

EDDIE: Amazing how much like Shakespeare Keats could be.
   (*They laugh again—but* JACK *has turned his attention on to the boy.*)

JACK: You know it, do you?
   (CLAYTON *shifts awkwardly, embarrassed.*)

CLAYTON: Ode To A Nightingale.

EDDIE: Tweet tweet.

JACK: (*Ignoring* EDDIE) Can you continue?

CLAYTON: Um. How do you mean—?

JACK: With the lines. The lines.

EDDIE: Leave the kid alone.
   (*But* CLAYTON *glares at his father, and then, with immense, strained concentration—*)

CLAYTON: Um. Fade far away—
   (*Then he stops, and looks at* LUCY, *almost longingly.*)

JACK: That's it. You've got it. Go on.

CLAYTON: Fade far away, dissolve, and quite forget
What thou among the leaves hast never known,
The weariness—um—

JACK: (*Harshly*)—the fever.

CLAYTON: The weariness, the fever, and the fret
Here—um—
Here, where men sit and hear each other groan;
Where palsy shakes a few, sad, last grey hairs,
Um—where—
(*He stops. He looks, again, at* LUCY. *Then drops his head. Little pause.*)

JACK: Where youth grows pale, and spectre-thin, and dies;
Where but to think is to be—

EDDIE: (*Joining in as* JACK *continues*)—full of sorrow
And leaden-eyed despairs;
(JACK *falls into astounded silence, and* EDDIE *continues, alone.*)
Where Beauty cannot keep her lustrous eyes,
Or new Love pine at them beyond to-morrow.
(*Pause.* JACK *realizes that* EDDIE *has been playing with him. He is upset, humiliated.*)

JACK: You bastard. You smart-arse.

EDDIE: That's OK, Jack. I still prefer a good balance sheet.
(*Then, from way out at sea, a plangent ship's hooter sounds.*)

LUCY: Oh, that sound.

ELIZABETH: It came right on cue.

EDDIE: (*Slight jeer*) Oh yeah? You think he heard us?

ELIZABETH: It always makes my skin crawl. That, and the whistle of a train.
(EDDIE *slaps at his arm again.*)

EDDIE: (*Slapping*) Why do the evil little bastards always pick on *me*!

LUCY: Perhaps they're literary critics.
(JACK*'s gaze is fixed hard on* CLAYTON. CLAYTON *fidgets, not liking it.*)

CLAYTON: What's the matter—?

JACK: What?
(CLAYTON *almost stands up in his anxiety.*)

CLAYTON: Why are you staring at me?

JACK: Do you *like* that poem? Does it say anything to you?
  (CLAYTON *stares back at him, then turns his head slightly aside.*)
CLAYTON: It—yeh—it kind of makes me feel—
  (*His words trail off.*)
JACK: Makes you feel what?
  (CLAYTON *looks directly at his father.* JACK *notices.*)
CLAYTON: Sad. It makes me feel sad.
JACK: (*relentless*) What sort of sad?
EDDIE: Come on. Is this an examination or something? Does he get a prize?
  (CLAYTON *stares at his father, ferociously.*)
CLAYTON: Sad because of the pain in the world. And the *dirt*. And *lies*. And the—(*He stops, controls himself.*) Sad. Just sad, I guess.
LUCY: Oh, but you're so *young*, Clayton. Don't feel that! You've got everything in front of you.
  (EDDIE *suddenly slaps himself again.*)
EDDIE: You'd think the cigar smoke would keep them off!
JACK: Melancholy is not a crime, Lucy. In fact, it's an act of mental hygiene. And there's absolutely no reason why it should be confined to the old and infirm. Or even (*Raises his glass.*) the seedily middle-aged.
  (*Even more distant, even more plangent, the ship's hooter sounds again. Tiny pause.*)
EDDIE: (*To* CLAYTON) You didn't tell me you liked that kind of stuff, Clay. Why didn't you stop me when I was talking with you this afternoon—?
  (CLAYTON *gives a faintly dismissive shrug.*)
CLAYTON: It doesn't matter.
  (EDDIE *laughs to cover his intense irritation.*)
EDDIE: Why do you always shrug like that when I'm talking to you?
JACK: Most people do, Eddie.
  (EDDIE *glares at* JACK, *who smirks.*)
EDDIE: (*Ignoring* JACK) Here's me telling Clayton about Sydney Sheldon and Arthur Hailey—can you imagine? Try them, I said. You can do worse than open a good meaty book now and then, I said.

(*They laugh, except* JACK.)

JACK: But that's good fatherly advice, Ed. I especially like the 'good meaty' bit. What do you tell him to eat? I'd really like to sit in on that conversation. Do you tell him which polysaccharide to put in the gravy?

EDDIE: O–ho. Here we go again.

ELIZABETH: Don't be a bore, Jack. There's a love.

LUCY: Why don't we go to the taverna? We could throw plates at each other.

JACK: It's too bloody far.

LUCY: It's only a mile along the beach—that's the quickest way. And the sea is so beautiful at night. Sort of—eerie.

JACK: Oh, I can get there all right. Just about. But who the hell is going to carry me back? *That* would be eerie. Besides, we've got gallons of wine here.

ELIZABETH: Not at the rate you're guzzling.

JACK: Have some more. Clayton—how about you? Eh? A little more, old lad.

(JACK *lurches toward the youth.*)

CLAYTON: No. Thank you.

JACK: Come on! A beaker full of the warm South. It blots out all the groans. Blanks out all the—

(CLAYTON *tries to put his hand over his glass.*)

EDDIE: (*Almost a snarl*) If he doesn't want it—

(CLAYTON *removes his hand.*)

CLAYTON: It's OK. I'll leave what I don't want.

JACK: Attaboy. Moderation is an intolerable vice. It's given me no end of trouble, I can tell you.

(*Finishing pouring,* JACK *ruffles* CLAYTON*'s hair with a slightly menacing* bonhomie, *the wine in his other hand.*)

CLAYTON: Don't do that. Please don't do that.

JACK: Aw, now—what's wrong? You think I'm queer or something?

CLAYTON: No. I just—don't like it, that's all.

(JACK *pulls a face, and returning to his chair, trips on the stone cube which, by day, holds the pole for a big parasol. He just retains his balance in a rather miraculous, prolonged stagger. And then sits with such composed, comical dignity that the others laugh.*)

31

EDDIE: He didn't even let go of the bottle!

ELIZABETH: I *told* you, Jack.

JACK: I'm sure you did. *What* did you tell me?

ELIZABETH: I said if you stood up you'd fall down.

JACK: Ah, but I didn't, did I? I retain complete control of all my faculties. (*Disdainful sniff*.) Except of course that of my taste buds. Which is invaluable in my work, of course.

ELIZABETH: Oh, God.

JACK: But you can't expect to work for Greenace and retain *those*, can you?

EDDIE: So you're still with us, are you?

JACK: (*Cautiously*) How do you mean?

EDDIE: It was my understanding that you had resigned this morning.

JACK: Oh, no. No, no. It's not going to be as easy as that. (*Peers at* EDDIE.) Is that what you want? Is that what's supposed to happen? You can't actually fire me, so you are given the job of persuading me to resign. Ho bloody ho ho.

LUCY: Why don't we go to the taverna? Who's willing?

ELIZABETH: I will. If you really want to. And if we really can throw the plates at each other.

LUCY: How about you, Clayton? Want to go?

CLAYTON: (*Unenthusiastic*) Sure.

JACK: Why don't you deal off the top of the pack, Eddie? Is that your brief? To provoke me into resigning. I wouldn't be a bit surprised. That's your sort of scheme. Oh, yes. Pity it won't work.

EDDIE: Just because we're all plotting against you is no reason to be paranoid, old pal.

LUCY: Let's go, for God's sake. Anything to get away.

ELIZABETH: Jack. Will you stop! Will you once and for all *stop*!

JACK: (*Mimicry*) 'It was my understanding that you had resigned this morning.'

EDDIE: That's OK, Jack. You threaten to resign at least once a month. Don't be too surprised if we take you up on it.
(JACK *goes to reply, then doesn't. Moodily, he twirls his wine glass in his hands.* EDDIE *slaps at a mosquito. Silence.*)

ELIZABETH: Oh, isn't this all such fun.

LUCY: (*Flat*) And the dish ran away with the spoon.

JACK: (*Heavily*) Clayton.

(CLAYTON *almost jumps.*)

CLAYTON: Yes?

JACK: You like Keats. And you don't like being touched. Is that a fair assessment?

CLAYTON: (*Cautiously*) Depends.

EDDIE: Leave him alone, Jack. You hear?

JACK: Clayton. Will you try to see the old black freighter, please?

CLAYTON: What?

JACK: In the morning. Try to see it in the morning.

CLAYTON: Why do you want me to? Isn't it yours?

JACK: No. You can have a glimpse of it, too. I'll give you a piece. No charge.

ELIZABETH: What are you talking about?

(JACK *ignores the question.*)

JACK: (*To* CLAYTON) I have the feeling that you *did* understand my sad little rhap—so—dy. Didn't you? This morning.

(CLAYTON *shifts awkwardly.*)

CLAYTON: Maybe.

JACK: Come on. You did. Didn't you?

CLAYTON: Maybe.

JACK: Then I'm sorry I talked down to you. Truly sorry, old lad, for being such a patronizing old fart. I didn't know there was a kindred soul suffering here under the same hot tiles.

EDDIE: I think we should all stick to doing what we do best. And it's not so easy to be a patronizing old fart. Don't apologize for it.

LUCY: I heard you talking about it, Jack. I'd like to see it, too.

EDDIE: See what?

LUCY: A ship that passes every morning.

EDDIE: What?

JACK: Very, very slowly.

EDDIE: Sounds real exciting. Where's it going to?

JACK: No, I don't suppose it would be worth your while to wake up especially to see it, Eddie. You're quite right. It's only going there and back.

(EDDIE *looks at him.*)

EDDIE: I don't know whether it would or not. What do you think, Clayton?

CLAYTON: Don't know.

EDDIE: Christ, if you shrug once more—! (*He stops, controls his tone.*) No. Of course you don't. Sorry.
(*An awkward little pause.*)

JACK: Actually, the bloody ship probably isn't there. A ship of fools. I probably didn't even see it. It was only a speck. A smudge on the horizon—or on the back of my eyelids.

ELIZABETH: A pink elephant, do you mean?
(*JACK raises his glass to her.*)

JACK: Exactly, my sweet.

LUCY: If we don't go soon, it won't be worth going at all. They'll start putting the chairs on the tables.

EDDIE: I don't think anyone really wants the taverna tonight, Lucy.

LUCY: But why not? It might put some life into us!

ELIZABETH: Impossible.
(*EDDIE suddenly, violently, slaps his arm again.*)

EDDIE: Goddamn bugs!

ELIZABETH: (*Laugh.*) They just *love* the taste of your blood, Eddie. You're *much* too sweet!
(*CLAYTON stands up, face dark, affected by the sensuality of her voice, even though it is masked by humour.*)

CLAYTON: I'm going to my room, OK?

LUCY: What's the matter, Clayton?

CLAYTON: (*Sudden yell*) What's the matter? What's the matter?
(*He stops, his voice changes.*) Lucy—are you blind. . . ?
(*They look at him, astonished. And CLAYTON's sudden rage deserts him, leaving him abandoned with his acute embarrassment. He looks at them, confused, then lopes away toward the stairs.*)

EDDIE: What was all *that* about?

LUCY: Oh, poor Clayton. This isn't much fun for him.

ELIZABETH: Why don't you leave him alone, Jack!

JACK: (*Astounded*) Me?

ELIZABETH: You're always getting at him. He doesn't understand your sarcasm, or your irony, or whatever you call it.

34

EDDIE: He's only a kid, Jack. And very young for his age. Stop needling him, will you!

JACK: Jesus Christ Almighty!

EDDIE: You can get at me as much as you want. But just leave off Clayton. Right? Or have you forgotten what it's like to be a kid of his age?

JACK: (*Still astounded*) What have I done? What have I said?

LUCY: No. It wasn't Jack. Not this time.

JACK: Too bloody right it wasn't!

EDDIE: Then what got into him? Why'd he flare up like that?

LUCY: Perhaps he doesn't like us. Maybe he doesn't care for what he sees. Or what he hears.

EDDIE: I tell you, I can't seem to get through to that kid. We don't seem to have any points of contact about anything.

LUCY: You have to give it time. And patience.

ELIZABETH: He doesn't really know you, does he? Be fair.

EDDIE: Suppose not. But—he can't keep his face still when I say anything to him. Now I know how Billy Graham must have felt when he had dinner with Nixon.

JACK: What does he want to do? I mean—what sort of career? Have you talked about it?

EDDIE: No. We haven't talked about *anything*. Lawyers shrug a lot, don't they? Maybe he should be a lawyer.

JACK: My father was a clergyman. When I asked him what sort of job I should do, he told me that it didn't particularly matter so long as I served Almighty God and refrained from excessive masturbation.

ELIZABETH: Then you should have taken his advice.

JACK: Oh, but I did. Until recently.

LUCY: He's very *wary* of everyone, Clayton is. He looks at you out of the corner of his eye.

EDDIE: Well, *I* don't know how to talk with him. He just kind of mutters and lowers his eyes. And bumps into things.

ELIZABETH: At least he's not *brash*. You've got to give him that.

LUCY: (*Looking at* EDDIE, *with an edge*) There's something there. There's something different about him. He's got a lot of sensitivity. He looks, and he sees. And he thinks.

EDDIE: *That*'ll help him a bundle. (*Provocative*) I said, that's no good to him. Unless he wants to be some kind of professor or something, walking about with his head down and a heap of books under his arm. It's great to make up little rhymes about nightingales or tomtits. But it won't pay the rent, will it?

JACK: That's disgustingly philistine—

EDDIE: Tweet tweet!

JACK: What?

EDDIE: I said—Tweet. Tweet.

ELIZABETH: Don't rise to the bait, Jack. Don't make a fool of yourself. Not again.

EDDIE: Tweet. Tweet.

JACK: Fuck off!

(EDDIE *pads across to* JACK, *with bottle and leer*.)

EDDIE: Have another drink, fella. Or is it *drinkie* you people say?

JACK: Who's 'you people'?

LUCY: Don't, Eddie. Please.

EDDIE: (*Pouring wine*) Why the hell not? Jack can take it. He's like London in the Blitz.

ELIZABETH: No, he can't. And no, he isn't. Except for the bomb sites.

JACK: And you're the bomb, darling.

LUCY: *Shut up!*

(*She says it with such vigour that they look at her*.)

ELIZABETH: (*Apologetic*) I know. I know.

JACK: Well, there's not much else to do, is there? I hate bloody holidays. Nothing to do in the daytime except get addled in the sun. Nothing to do at night except to go to sleep. Or, rather, lie there all sweaty on top of the bed, listening to my wife snore.

EDDIE: Oh, she *snores*, does she?

ELIZABETH: I do not!

JACK: Not one of those big, thunderous, vibrant, bellowing snores, I grant you. Nothing so honest or wholesome. It's more like the regular plop–plop of someone in a pair of rubber boots walking across a farmyard that's covered in cowshit.

(*He imitates noise, disgustingly*. LUCY *laughs*.)

36

ELIZABETH: Jack. You're a liar.

EDDIE: This changes everything, Elizabeth. I see you with new eyes now.

LUCY: Eddie snores, too.

EDDIE: I wouldn't be surprised. Emphatically, I hope.

JACK: Let snorer cleave unto snorer. Loud thunder unto snotty bubble. That's what I say.

ELIZABETH: But I don't. I'm sure I don't. This is slander.

JACK: Don't *you* think it's a good idea, Lucy? The snorers in the same room at nights?

(*Fractional pause.*)

LUCY: I don't think *that* would be the reason, Jack.

(*Fractional pause.* EDDIE *and* ELIZABETH *avoid looking at each other.*)

JACK: No, it's not good enough reason in itself, I agree. But we could make it the reason for accepting the reason, so to speak.

EDDIE: What are you saying here, Jack?

(*Fractional pause.*)

JACK: Nothing. Nothing.

(*Then* JACK *looks at* LUCY.)

LUCY: Don't look at *me*, buster.

EDDIE: (*Aware of tension*) Lucy—?

JACK: (*Cutting in*) Higamus, Hogamus, Woman is monogamous
Hogamus, Higamus, Man is polygamous.

End of quote.

ELIZABETH: *Some* men, Jack. Half the time you're too drunk even to *find* the bed.

JACK: Quite so, my dear. Quite so. My vital equipment is well and truly pickled. I'm as limp as a piece of airline celery. You know, the kind that leaks into your Bloody Mary.

(EDDIE *emits an awkward little laugh.*)

EDDIE: I don't believe it.

ELIZABETH: Oh, but it's true!

(JACK *studies her. A silence.*)

JACK: Is that why you think you have to look elsewhere?

ELIZABETH: What?

JACK: (*Mimic*) 'They just *love* the taste of your blood, Eddie.

You're *much* too sweet!' Guess who's coming to dinner. And it's not a mosquito—is it?

EDDIE: What are you getting at?

ELIZABETH: He's just being his usual self, Eddie. Don't rise to it. Please.

EDDIE: I don't like these innuendoes. I'm too old, and it's too late.

LUCY: He prefers something more specific.

EDDIE: What?

LUCY: And I agree with you, Eddie. Jack—what are you trying to say? Is it the same thing *I*'d like to say?

EDDIE: Hey—what *is* this—?

ELIZABETH: Yes. What are you on about?

LUCY: Oh, listen to them, Jack. Don't they make a sweet couple?

JACK: Blue-eyed and innocent.

EDDIE: Now, listen—

JACK: (*Quickly—more a cry*) Don't let's talk about it! Please don't let's talk about—
(*Silence.*)

ELIZABETH: Talk about *what*, though?
(EDDIE *remains silent, and tries to shake his head at* ELIZABETH.)

LUCY: Yes, Jack. Now that we've almost opened the door—what do *you* want to talk about?
(*Silence.*)

JACK: The ship.

ELIZABETH: What?

JACK: The freighter that—(*He is upset.*)—that passes every morning.

LUCY: Well—why not? Let's talk about your freighter. You're right. It's better than discussing the ships that pass in the night.

EDDIE: Are you crazy? Are you two crazy—? I don't know what you are hinting at, Lucy, but you're way off base.
(*Silence.* LUCY *stares at* EDDIE. ELIZABETH *hangs her head. Then* LUCY *turns to* JACK, *her tone more gentle.*)

LUCY: What time do you see it, Jack? This boat of yours.

JACK: At—at about half-past five.

LUCY: Then it's a date. I'll see it with you.

38

(*Pause.* EDDIE *and* ELIZABETH, *unwisely, look at each other.*)

EDDIE: We—ah—we'll all see it—

ELIZABETH: Yes! I'd like that!

(*Her false enthusiasm causes another small silence.* EDDIE, *strained, suddenly slaps at his arm again.*)

EDDIE: They're driving me mad, these insects! I'll have to go inside.

(*Then* JACK *makes a little, helpless, choking sound, less than a sob, more than a word.*)

JACK: Elizabeth.

(*She reacts like one shot, and stands up, rigid.*)

ELIZABETH: I'm going to bed. I'm not staying out here.

(JACK *looks down into his glass.*)

LUCY: (*Stiffly*) Goodnight, then. Goodnight.

(EDDIE *slaps his glass down, and lurches to his feet.*)

EDDIE: OK! OK! OK! Fuck you both!

LUCY: Which two do you mean, hon–ey?

EDDIE: Wait for me, Elizabeth. I'm coming with you.

(ELIZABETH *hesitates. Then—*)

ELIZABETH: I—yes. All right.

(*But then they both hesitate.*)

LUCY: Go on, then! Go! Get out!

(EDDIE *half shrugs, then, holding* ELIZABETH *by the elbow, leads or propels her away. Silence.* JACK *and* LUCY *do not look at each other. Then* LUCY *giggles—bitterly.*)

LUCY: Which room will they use, do you reckon? Ours—or yours?

(JACK, *rigid, stares into his glass. Then he lifts his head and looks at her.*)

JACK: What did you say?

LUCY: Nothing.

JACK: (*Almost vacantly*) What?

LUCY: I didn't say anything, Jack. There isn't anything to say. We know now, don't we? Don't we just!

(*Silence. They do not move. Then* JACK *suddenly slaps at a mosquito or insect on the back of his neck. Silence. Then—*)

I feel tired. But I don't quite know which room to go to.

JACK: Why not give young Clayton a thrill?

39

LUCY: Don't be nasty. Please.
> (*Pause. Then* JACK *twists his head away.*)

JACK: If I lose her, Lucy—
> (*He doesn't finish.*)

LUCY: This is *so* ridiculous!
> (*She gets up. And then sits down again.*)
>
> I don't know what to do. I just don't–know–what–to–do.
> (*She looks at him.*) Eddie says you kick the radiators.

JACK: What?

LUCY: At work. Eddie said you were so mad after some policy meeting or something that you went along the corridor kicking the radiators.

JACK: Yes. That's right. I did. And hurt my foot.

LUCY: Did it help any?

JACK: (*Sepulchral*) No—o—o.
> (*Despite herself, she half laughs. Then—*)

LUCY: It all came up out of nowhere. I'd shut my eyes to it. The thing between Eddie and—I think it was Clayton asking if I was blind. Suddenly, I—oh God. I didn't know. I didn't really know until, suddenly, I *did* know. (*Looks at* JACK.) I think I'll sit out here all night. Why not? Just stay here. All night long.

JACK: And wait for the ship.

LUCY: And wait for morning.

JACK: That's what we're all doing anyway. Waiting for the boat.

LUCY: What? Oh. Yes. In a way. (*Then looks at him.*) Don't be so morbid.

JACK: I used to have to listen to an enormous number of extremely turgid hymns when I was a boy. My father was low church. (*Sigh.*) Very evangelical. An awful lot of those bloody dirges were about the boat crossing over to the other shore. On the far side of the Jordan. Where all our loved ones were waiting—the ones who've gone before. What a bloody thought!

LUCY: Ain't it.

JACK: Do you know what's *really* there? On the far side of the Jordan. (*Sniff.*) Refugees.

LUCY: And terrorists.

(*Pause. They look at each other.*)

JACK: You can't really blame Elizabeth, you know.

LUCY: Oh but I do! The bitch! Don't start being *noble*.

(*He sighs, then finishes his glass of wine.*)

JACK: I'm not, I assure you. Not at all. I haven't got the resolve
to be anything very much, one way or the other. My Yea is
not exactly a Yea, and my Nay is very rarely a Nay. I'm
English, you see. I'm helplessly, compromisingly bloody
well damned well English.

LUCY: That's nothing to do with it—

JACK: My hot is not hot and my cold is not cold. Just a sort of
lukewarm grey sludge. Indistinguishable, I should imagine,
from the colour of vomit.

LUCY: You're enjoying this, aren't you! You *love* feeling sorry for
yourself. God—you're a creep!

JACK: I'm talking about this dank little room bob-bobbing about
on top of my shoulders. The inside of my head, darling. I'd
give a lot to find a suitable tenant, but there's none to be
had.

LUCY: Eddie's right! Somebody should light a fire under your
ass!

JACK: Damp twigs don't burn, duckie.

(*He simpers, sadly pleased with himself. But then his expression
changes. And, just as she is about to speak—*)

I did something this morning that I never imagined for one
moment that I would do.

LUCY: What are we going to do? Jack—?

JACK: The ship had just gone out of sight. There was only the
faintest plume of smoke from its stack, and even that was
merging with the sky. I couldn't make out what was the sea
and what was the sky, anyway. They were the same,
opaque, oddly ethereal substance, as clean and as empty as
the new day. (*He hiccups.*) Pardon me. The waters which
were under the firmament and the waters which were above
the firmament, as my gaga old daddy would have put it.
(*Hiccups again, and then strikes his chest.*) Shit! 'And the
evening and the morning were the second day.' Oh, yes, I
thought. Here we are, just as at the beginning—when the

41

world was so new there was scarcely a line between heaven and earth. A bird, little brown bird, came and perched on the olive tree just below me. (*Sort of hiccups, or gasps, again, and it seems a bit painful.*) Damn! It opened its throat and it sang—There was—do you know, there was nothing between me and all that out there—the sea, the sky, the bird, the tree—nothing except my own—(*Gasps.*)—my own sour, tired disappointment and—Oh–h–h–h—And then I had this sense of wonder. No, of expectation. A tension. I don't know. But I was *waiting.*(*He sucks in his breath, suddenly, as though in pain.*) I thought to myself—Perhaps it's all going to come back. The wonderful, wonderful belief I had as a child. The *overwhelming* comfort of knowing that Everything Was All Right, because God was there, and God looked after the world, like a gardener would.

(*He stops. His whole posture seems to droop with a great weight.*)

LUCY: Jack?

(*A moment. Then he looks up at her.*)

JACK: And so I said to myself—Hold still. Keep quiet. Don't move. Don't think. Most of all, don't get down on your knees, and don't ask for anything. Wait—just wait. And if, after all, after everything, if there is, is, really is, truly is a God, a loving God in his loving Creation, then he will reveal himself between the bones of my head.

All I had to do was *wait.*

And I waited. For the word. The sense.

Watching the very last traces of smoke from the old black freighter, as far away as the eye could see.

And—

Nothing came.

(*He slaps at his chest-bone again, in discomfort and his voice is thicker.*)

No. Worse. Something came, winging across the water, or dropping out of the sky, from everywhere, all around me, inside my nose and at the back of my throat. I could smell it and taste it. Disgust. It was disgust. Nausea. Rotting, slimy, stench. The maggoty corpse of—what?

Guess what. Guess who.

(*Pause. Then, like a child, unprotected and defenceless to the emotion, he begins, openly, to weep.* LUCY, *unsure, goes toward him, hovers a little, then, in a sudden compulsive movement, she tries to put her arms around him.*)

LUCY: Jack. Jack. Oh, don't. Don't.

(*Crying, he seems at first to yield to her compulsive, compassionate embrace. But then he pushes her away, hard.*)

JACK: Get off! Leave me be!

LUCY: OK. OK!

(*Astonishingly, he lurches after her, hand raised.*)

JACK: You interfering bitch! It was *you* that brought it all out— Him and Her—the *bastards*—

LUCY: Jack—!

(*But in the momentum of his sudden fury he slaps out at her. Astonished, they look at each other. Then he drops his head.*)

JACK: I'm sorry. I'm—sorry.

(*She just stands there, looking at him evenly. He goes to turn away, ashamed. And then, in a sudden bellow of pain and rage, he whirls back—*)

(*Yell*) No I'm not! No—o!

(*And at the same time he hits her, so hard that she is knocked down. Aghast, he stands over her.*)

I'm—Lucy. I'm sorry. I'm so sorry.

LUCY: (*Gasp*) That's all you ever say—that's all you're capable of saying . . .

JACK: Yes!

LUCY: Eddie never says sorry. He's—(*Starts to cry*)—He's one hell of a guy. You just don't know him. He's the smartest man I ever met—

JACK: No—o—o!

(*And he drives his foot into her. She yelps. He stops himself, shocked, and goes to pull her up.*)

LUCY: Get away! Don't touch me!

(*She lies still. He stands still. The light fades. In near darkness—*)

JACK: I'm sorry, Lucy. I'm so—sorry.

ACT TWO

The next morning, which is a Sunday.

   EDDIE *and* ELIZABETH *are sprawled on sun loungers under the big bright parasol on the terrace. She is rubbing suntan oil on her legs. She seems sullen, withdrawn, self-absorbed. He is in flowery shorts and sandals, morosely sipping a cold drink.*

   He looks at her, goes to speak, then doesn't. Apparently troubled, and with a mannered sigh calculated to get a response from her, he ostentatiously looks at his wristwatch.

EDDIE: Ten o'clock. Already.
   (*She doesn't answer. Pause.*)
   What are those two trying to pull? Why don't they get up?
   Haven't they had enough of each other?
   (*She doesn't answer. Pause.*)
   What the hell do they think they're doing?
   (*Still no response.*)
   Listen to those goddamn crickets, or whatever. Cicadas.
   Don't they ever stop! (*Looks at her.*) Elizabeth. What's
   happening? Are they going to stay in bed all day—?
   (*She doesn't answer.*)
   Jeez! They must be enjoying it! (*Looks at her, then, savagely*)
   What the hell's wrong with you? Swallowed some suntan
   oil?
ELIZABETH: Nothing whatsoever.
EDDIE: You're acting like we're married already!
ELIZABETH: That'll be the day!
EDDIE: What's wrong with you? Why don't you answer?
ELIZABETH: By the way, you *do* snore.
EDDIE: And so do you, honey. Just like Jack said!
   (*Pause. Then she laughs, but not amiably.*)
ELIZABETH: You're such a fool, Eddie.
EDDIE: What?
ELIZABETH: 'Wait for me, Elizabeth. I'm coming with you.'

What did you do it for? So blatant! They didn't *really* know. It would have been much more civilized to have left things as they were.

EDDIE: Of course they knew!

ELIZABETH: *Jack* didn't. He wouldn't know if you took his socks off him while he was still wearing them.

EDDIE: He knew, all right. What do you think he was talking about? I should have known he was on to something when he went crazy about dipping bananas. He's got a very complicated mind, that Jack.

ELIZABETH: He was just thrashing around, trying to get at you. That's his style. Jack's accused me of having it off with half a dozen different chaps—and they're all enemies of his.

EDDIE: And have you?

ELIZABETH: That's my business. Hold your tongue, please.

EDDIE: I would if it wasn't all furred up.

(*Pause. He looks at his watch again.*)

ELIZABETH: It's no use you looking at your watch all the time. They're enjoying themselves.

EDDIE: You think so?

ELIZABETH: (*Amused*) Well, maybe *she* isn't. Novelty isn't always the aphrodisiac it's cracked up to be.

EDDIE: Takes two to tango, baby.

ELIZABETH: She didn't waste much time, did she? I bet she practically carried poor old Jack up the stairs.

EDDIE: Maybe it was the other way around. I've noticed the gleam in 'poor old' Jack's eye.

ELIZABETH: You must be joking! The most he'd ever *dare* do is peep down the front of her blouse.

EDDIE: Well, he's done more than that now.

ELIZABETH: What's going to happen, Eddie? How's it all going to work out?

EDDIE: (*Cautiously*) You and me?

ELIZABETH: You and me. And me and him. And you and her.

EDDIE: You left out Him and Her.

ELIZABETH: What's going to happen? What are we going to do?

EDDIE: Get a bigger bed, I suppose.

ELIZABETH: I don't think we're going to be able to keep it as a joke. Hilarious though it is.

EDDIE: (*Cautiously*) What do *you* want, Elizabeth?

ELIZABETH: Me? I'd like to cut someone's balls off. The question is—whose?

EDDIE: Don't look at *me* like that!

ELIZABETH: Jack probably talked all night long. About mono-sodium glutamate. And serve her right!

EDDIE: Oh no he didn't. This is for real. Pure wholemeal.

ELIZABETH: I don't know. Is it?

EDDIE: (*Laugh.*) You'd better believe it. I can hear the lawyers galloping toward us, bugles blowing, flags flying.

ELIZABETH: Maybe it's the sun. Or all that wine we drank. But it feels utterly ridiculous.

EDDIE: That's for sure. I hate things out in the open. The snipers get you that way.

(*Behind them,* CLAYTON *is coming down the stairs. They cannot see him. There is something even more hesitant—and rather oddly furtive—about his physical manner. He hangs back.*)

ELIZABETH: Listen, if we *all* behave as though it *was* a game— mmm? As though nothing much happened. It's a good way of dealing with things. Sort of pretend it never happened. Jack's very good at shutting his eyes to things.

EDDIE: Yeh. It's *words* that bother him. Which Thesaurus shall we use?

ELIZABETH: Depends on what everybody wants. One drunken, *boring* night on a Greek island we changed partners— Driven mad by mosquitoes, we hopped into the wrong beds. Almost by accident, so to speak—

CLAYTON: Hi.

EDDIE: (*Adjusting*) Hi, Clayton. How's things?

ELIZABETH: Good morning.

(CLAYTON *looks at them, stiffly shy.*)

CLAYTON: Um. Dad—

EDDIE: Yes?

(CLAYTON *suddenly turns half away, furtive.*)

CLAYTON: Look at that sea. Aren't those colours something?

EDDIE: Yeh. Pretty neat. Clayton—is something wrong—?

(CLAYTON *looks at them, then his eyes plunge away again.*)

46

CLAYTON: You wouldn't know there were so many different kinds of blue. If you hadn't seen it for yourself.

(EDDIE *and* ELIZABETH *exchange quick glances.*)

EDDIE: Did you—ah—did you sleep well, son? I mean—ah—

CLAYTON: It's as though blue was the *only* colour, and had to stand in for all the others.

EDDIE: What?

CLAYTON: (*Strained*) There's a red blue, an orange blue, a yellow blue. A green blue. A blue blue. An indigo blue. And—(*He stops.*)—Dad? I mean—Father?

EDDIE: Yes?

CLAYTON: It's *clean* out there.

(*Awkward little pause.* EDDIE *feels he is being accused.*)

EDDIE: What are you trying to say, Clayton?

CLAYTON: I'm not trying to say anything. I'm just telling you it's clean out there. And blue.

EDDIE: Yeh. I got that. Especially the blue.

(*He tries to laugh. But* CLAYTON *is staring at them.*)

ELIZABETH: We all had rather too much to drink last night, and—we're not too keen on blue at the moment.

CLAYTON: (*Abrupt*) What's for breakfast?

EDDIE: No idea. It's Sunday. The cook doesn't come today. What do you want? Something with blue in it, I guess.

ELIZABETH: We have to fend for ourselves today. Somebody had better lock away the knives, though.

(CLAYTON *continues to stare at them.*)

EDDIE: For Christ's sake, Clay. You make me feel I got two heads or something. What's the *matter*?

CLAYTON: I think I'll scramble some eggs.

ELIZABETH: You want me to do it—? So long as I only use a spoon.

CLAYTON: (*Hostile*) Do I want *you* to do it?

EDDIE: Hey! Hey!

(CLAYTON *walks abruptly away, toward kitchen.*)

Clayton!

ELIZABETH: Leave it, Eddie. Leave it.

(CLAYTON *has gone into kitchen.*)

EDDIE: What the hell is wrong with him! First off, he creeps up

47

behind us and talks about *blue* like he'd never seen it before, and then he stares at *me* like he's never seen it before.

ELIZABETH: He's the sort of boy who listens at doors. Haven't you noticed his very flat ears?

EDDIE: What?

ELIZABETH: Bedroom doors, darling.

EDDIE: Oh, God. You think—? Hell! I should never have invited him along. He's getting nothing out of this vacation. Nothing he needs, that's for sure.

ELIZABETH: Well, what did you ask him for? He just moons around looking miserable. Christ, don't you absolutely loathe the very young? I do!

EDDIE: I've seen him three—no, four times in the last three years. Since I moved to England with Greenace. I don't know him any more. And I'm damned sure his mother has prejudiced him against me—Hell, he can hardly look me straight in the face. Where are you going?

ELIZABETH: To see about his breakfast, of course. I'm not a liberated woman. Or haven't you noticed?

EDDIE: Try to *talk* with him. Find out what's bugging him, will you?

ELIZABETH: He'll probably throw the eggs at me.
(*As she turns to go, she stops dead—*LUCY *is coming down the stairs. And* LUCY, *too, stops momentarily, then continues on down.*)

EDDIE: What is it—?

ELIZABETH: It's Lucy. She—(*Astonished*) She's got a black eye!
(ELIZABETH *goes toward* LUCY, *and* EDDIE *follows, gaping.*)

LUCY: Good morning, folks. Did you catch the Big Fight last night?

EDDIE: Lucy—what the—

ELIZABETH: That *is* a black eye I see. Isn't it?

LUCY: Happened in the third round.

EDDIE: *How'd* it happen?

LUCY: Jack did it. In his passion. I had no idea he wanted me so much.
(*Tiny, comical pause.*)

EDDIE: You're kidding.

ELIZABETH: I don't believe it. Jack couldn't.

48

LUCY: Oh, yes he could. 'Poor old Jack' packs one hell of a punch, believe you me. He kicks pretty well, too. You should see my ribs.

EDDIE: You don't mean it—?

LUCY: But I do.

(*She looks at them. A moment—then* EDDIE *starts up the stairs, enraged.*)

EDDIE: I'll break his neck, the bastard—

LUCY: Where you going?

EDDIE: Where d'you think—the fucking pervert—!

LUCY: He's not there. He never was there.

(EDDIE *stops in mid-stride.*)

EDDIE: What—?

ELIZABETH: Then where is he? What's happened to him?

LUCY: He's probably floating face-down on the sea by now.

ELIZABETH: No, no. He doesn't drink water.

LUCY: He hit me and kicked me and knocked me down, out there on the terrace. Then he picked me up, hugged me, cried a little, and (*shrug*) *ran off*.

EDDIE: Where to?

LUCY: Into the night.

(CLAYTON *stands at the kitchen door, watching, listening.*)

ELIZABETH: I don't believe you. He never *runs* anywhere.

EDDIE: Why'd he hit you—has he gone crazy?

LUCY: Probably. No—amend that. *Certainly.*

ELIZABETH: Christ, what a bore! Think he's done himself in?

EDDIE: No. Of course not. He wouldn't!

LUCY: He might. I wouldn't be surprised.

(ELIZABETH *laughs, but a little uneasily.*)

ELIZABETH: Why didn't you tell us?

LUCY: I didn't want to interrupt your fun and games. I might have come in slap in the middle of your second orgasm, mightn't I?

EDDIE: Shut up, Lucy. Please.

(*He has become aware of* CLAYTON.)

ELIZABETH: *Second* orgasm? You could have knocked during the first, darling. And still beat the dawn.

EDDIE: (*Soft hiss*) Jesus Christ. Shut up, will you!

(ELIZABETH *hides a growing anxiety.*)

ELIZABETH: Well, I suppose we'd better look for the silly bugger. Why is he such a bore?

LUCY: Oh, I see. You had nothing to do with any of this, Elizabeth. You didn't go to bed with my husband after all.

ELIZABETH: Oh, come on. We were all too drunk to notice.

(EDDIE *is looking anxiously at seemingly impassive* CLAYTON.)

EDDIE: We don't have to talk about it *now*, do we? I mean—

ELIZABETH: No. We'd better search for Jack. Perhaps his fist is bleeding.

CLAYTON: (*Suddenly*) And supposing he's dead? What if he's drowned himself?

(*Then all look at him.* CLAYTON *looks at them, then bolts back into the safety of the kitchen.* LUCY *starts to laugh: the kind of laugh which shows she is not cool at all.*)

EDDIE: What's so funny?

LUCY: Jack. Maybe he *has*. It's the kind of dignified thing he'd do.

ELIZABETH: It is, actually. Yes.

(*She, too, laughs. But then they stop, anxiety intruding.*)

EDDIE: OK. OK we'll look for him. We'll go look.

LUCY: Not me. I'm not.

ELIZABETH: Coward.

LUCY: It must be miles to the nearest cuckoo house. But I'm sure that's where you'll find him.

EDDIE: Lucy—did he *say* anything—? Have you any idea where he's gone, or what he's playing at?

ELIZABETH: He must have said *something*—

LUCY: Well. Yes. He kicked me his farewell kick. In the ribs. And then he yelled—um—what was it? Famous last words, 'Mushrooms are Magic!' Or something like that—

ELIZABETH: What?

LUCY: Mushrooms are magic.

(EDDIE *expels his breath.*)

EDDIE: He's flipped. He's finally flipped.

ELIZABETH: We've got to search for him, Eddie. There's no telling what he's done.

EDDIE: OK. OK but—

ELIZABETH: Naturally, I shall hold the company responsible. How much would they fork out on a death-in-service policy?

EDDIE: OK OK! But I don't know where to look—

ELIZABETH: (*Departing*) We'll go down to the beach. We'll start there. And along the path to the taverna. If we keep calling his name he might even recognize it.

EDDIE: (*Departing*) He's probably lying on his back in the taverna, with retsina coming out of his ears—

(*They have gone.* LUCY *stands still. Expressionless. Then she puts her hand to her eye.*)

LUCY: (*Softly*) Poor old Jack.

(*Pause. Then* CLAYTON *reappears in the kitchen doorway, hesitant. From offstage, cries of* Jack!; Jack—*where are you!* LUCY *looks at* CLAYTON. *He swivels his head, lowers his eyes.*)

CLAYTON: Oh, Lucy.

LUCY: Clayton. I want to talk to you. I want you to listen to me.

CLAYTON: You are so beautiful.

LUCY: I didn't know what I was doing last night, Clayton. Can we sort of—forget it happened, or—

CLAYTON: Don't say that. Please. Never say that.

(*She looks at him, bites her lip.*)

LUCY: Clayton. Listen. I'm sorry, very sorry. When I came into your room, I—I sort of needed to hide, Clayton.

CLAYTON: (*Not listening*) You are so very beautiful. The most beautiful—

LUCY: (*Quickly*) I was getting at Eddie. I wanted to punish him!

(*Little pause. He freezes.*)

CLAYTON: What?

LUCY: It—it shouldn't have happened, Clayton. I was—I feel very ugly, inside. I'm very sorry. I—Please forgive me.

CLAYTON: Don't say that.

LUCY: Listen to me. Please. I was not myself. I was hurt—in all ways. And I—well, it's not a pleasant thing to say, but I was full of hate and—

CLAYTON: You didn't *mean* it? Any of it?

(*He is stiffening in potential hostility. She puts out a hand to touch him, then drops it.*)

51

LUCY: I'll always be grateful to you, always, Clayton. You are a
gentle and sensitive and—When I put my arms around you
in the dark, and cried like that, I *needed* someone to hold
me. But—oh, I'm sorry. I'm so sorry.

CLAYTON: You didn't mean it. That's what you're saying. You
used me just to get at—You used me.

(*He turns away, abrupt, and she catches at his arm.*)

LUCY: Don't turn away like that! I'm not trying to hurt you—

CLAYTON: You think it was *ugly*—?

LUCY: No, Clayton. Not in that way. No, of course not. I'm—
Clayton. Please don't get it out of—out of proportion. I—

CLAYTON: But what you are saying is—you don't love me. Right?

LUCY: L–love you? Oh, but—

(CLAYTON *suddenly, even roughly, grabs at her. His adolescent
fervour, touchingly comic, boils over, imploringly.*)

CLAYTON: Say you do. Say you do! Please say you do. Don't be
scared of it. I'm *old* enough. I can look out for you!

LUCY: Clayton. You're—this is silly—

CLAYTON: I keep saying your name. In my head. Lucy. Lucy.
Lucy. Over and over. It was like—it jumped up inside me.
When I first saw you. And you knew it, didn't you? You're
not like the others. You *knew* what I felt, I didn't know
where to put my eyes—!

LUCY: Oh, Clayton. You've got this all—

CLAYTON: When you left my room in the middle of the night and
you closed the door so quietly I could see your shape in the
light from the passage—and then the band of light
narrowing, as the door closed, the light narrowing, and
then it was dark—(*Suddenly, comically*)—
I cannot see what flowers are at my feet,
    Nor what soft incense hangs upon the boughs,
But, in embalmèd darkness, guess each sweet
    Wherewith the seasonable month endows . . .
(LUCY *puts her hands to her temples.*)

LUCY: Oh, God. Don't be so literate, Clayton.

CLAYTON: And in the dark, Lucy, there was your name. And I
said it over and over until the room was light again. (*Looks
at her.*) And you know what?

LUCY: Don't say any more. (*Tries a laugh.*) It might be in rhyme.

CLAYTON: I said it so much, your name, that it's *everywhere* now.

LUCY: Clayton. You're a nice boy, and—Clayton! You're
hypnotizing yourself. You're making all this up, and—

CLAYTON: It's in every room, your name, the sense of you. It's
hanging in the air. It's even out there over the sea,
mingling with the blue. (*Looks at her, comical little pause.*) Are
you going to kiss me, or not? That's what I want to know.
Yes or no.

LUCY: Clayton—

CLAYTON: Are you going to sort of flutter the tip of your tongue
in the corner of my lips—

LUCY: What?

CLAYTON: There's a lot you can teach me, Lucy. I've read the
Kama Sutra, you know. But that's theory, and—

LUCY: (*Wanting to laugh*) Clayton. Please come and sit down. I
want to talk to you—

CLAYTON: Tu es mon amour, ma chérie. Toujours. Je t'aime
avec tout mon coeur.

LUCY: (*Blink*) What?

CLAYTON: There's this tradition over there, see. An older
woman, more experienced—excuse me, I'm not being
rude—and a young man who's a—I beg your
pardon—well, a virgin. You follow me? And she *worships*
him, and cherishes him, and he sort of restores her to life.
Does that sound fair?
(*Almost as an answer, a loud and, in the circumstances, comical
groan rends the air.*)
(*Startled*) What was that—?

LUCY: I don't know. Maybe it's a wounded Frenchman.
(*The joke is lost on* CLAYTON. *Adolescent, he now dreads the
possibility that he was overheard.*)

CLAYTON: Is somebody there? Is somebody *listening*? Oh, God.
Did somebody *hear* us?
(*The loud, painful, exaggerated groan again.* LUCY *goes toward its
source: the low stone wall at the side of the terrace.*)

LUCY: I've got a good idea who—
(*She stops. A pair of hands grapple at the top of the wall. And then*

the head of JACK.)

My God. An Extra-Terrestrial.

(JACK *pulls himself over the little wall, heavily, and slumps down on to the near side, his back against the stone wall. He looks very much the worse for wear.* CLAYTON *and* LUCY *look at him.* JACK *groans, heartfelt.*)

JACK: Oh–h–h–h!

LUCY: Jack—what on earth are you doing?

CLAYTON: Were you *listening* to me?

(JACK *looks up at them, exhausted.*)

JACK: Do you think you could go so far as to help me up?

(*They don't.*)

LUCY: Where have you been? They're out searching for you.

JACK: Where've I been? Where've I bloody been? On the other side of the wall, that's where. On the bloody rocks—like a mermaid.

CLAYTON: When you get up, I'm going to knock you down!

JACK: Oh, thanks very much.

LUCY: Clayton. Leave it.

CLAYTON: Beating and kicking a woman! You're a wild animal. It's about time you got yours! Come on. Stand up!

JACK: Very well. I shall just sit here.

LUCY: We were sort of half hoping you'd drowned yourself.

JACK: Well, I'll tell you. I wouldn't mind a nice cup of tea.

LUCY: Go make him one, Clayton.

CLAYTON: What? *Him?*

JACK: You can knock me down afterwards, old son.

CLAYTON: Anybody who treats women like you do—

LUCY: Clayton. Be a good boy. I want to talk to Jack.

CLAYTON: (*Offended*) What?

JACK: Come on, old lad. Be a sport, eh? My mouth is like the bottom of a budgerigar's cage.

(CLAYTON *looks at* LUCY, *then at* JACK.)

CLAYTON: OK. Bastard.

(*He lopes away, sullen, then, before reaching kitchen, calls back—*)

And I hope it chokes you.

(*Little pause.* JACK *tries to smile up at her.*)

JACK: (*Croak*) Lucy.

54

LUCY: Are you just going to lie there? Do you know what you *look* like?

JACK: Something the cat brought in. But that's nothing to how I feel. (*As he moves a little*) Ouch—!

LUCY: (*Dubious*) Are you *really* hurt—?

JACK: I don't know. I've been lying on the rocks, with those horrible green lizards or whatever. Something very nasty crawled into my mouth.

LUCY: That's strange. Something very nasty usually crawls *out*.

JACK: Don't be unkind, Lucy.

(*She snorts with amusement.*)

LUCY: Have you seen my eye, Jack!

(*He looks up at her, and, almost puzzled, shakes his head.*)

JACK: Give me a hand, Lucy. There's a love.

(*She holds off a moment, he looks at her. Then, with a faint shrug, she puts her hand under his arm, and he gets to his feet, with difficulty.*)

LUCY: Come on. Get out of the sun, you silly old fool.

(*He sways, as though about to fall down, and clutches at her arm, contrite.*)

JACK: I hit you. Didn't I? Lucy, I hit you.

LUCY: I'll say you did.

JACK: Something seemed to—to—Oh, I'm sorry. I'm so sorry!

LUCY: (*Wry*) Perhaps you thought I was a radiator.

JACK: What?

(*She takes his arm, to lead him to a recliner, under the parasol.*)

LUCY: Come on. Sit down. You old fool. You poor old fool.

JACK: (*Shuffling across*) Is she going to leave me? Is he going to take her away? Lucy?

LUCY: I've no idea.

(JACK *plumps down on the recliner like a sack of potatoes.*)

JACK: I think I'm covered in bruises. It was pitch black beyond the terrace, and I went arse over tit on to those bloody rocks.

LUCY: Where were you going?

JACK: (*Airily*) Oh, to drown myself, of course. To cease upon the midnight, not exactly with no pain, but to cease anyway.

(LUCY *sits on the edge of the lounger, and looks at him.*)

LUCY: You're not serious. Are you?

JACK: When I've had my cup of tea.

(*Little pause. They seem to examine each other.*)

LUCY: Eddie and—Elizabeth are out looking for you.

JACK: Do you think they'll find me? Will they look under the right stone? I've been looking for me for years. Hope they have better luck. (*Disdainful sniff.*) You know what I dislike about holidays? Nothing ever happens. I didn't even see the ship that's supposed to pass in the night.

(LUCY *smiles. Then, on a sudden impulse, she leans in over him, and kisses him, chastely.*)

LUCY: Poor old Jack.

JACK: Bless you, Lucy.

(*She cups his face in her hands, and kisses him, less chastely.* CLAYTON, *returning with the tea, sees this, and stops so abruptly that the cup rattles in the saucer.*)

JACK: Ah. The tea.

LUCY: (*A little embarrassed*) Thank you, Clayton.

(*But* CLAYTON *stands stock still, face tight.*)

JACK: Hurry it up, old chap. Save a life, eh?

(*But* CLAYTON *does not move.*)

CLAYTON: I don't get you people!

LUCY: Clayton?

CLAYTON: I don't understand you! You *kissing* him and—ach! You make me sick to the stomach!

(LUCY, *concerned, gets up.*)

LUCY: Clayton—for goodness' sakes, you've got it all—

CLAYTON: You've no respect for anybody or anything, none of you! You're dirty! All of you! Dirty!

(*Unable to control, let alone understand, his own strong emotions, he hurls the cup to the floor, where it shatters. Aghast,* CLAYTON *looks at* LUCY—*then, with a suppressed sob of humiliation, turns and rushes off.* LUCY *goes to follow*—)

LUCY: Clayton—!

(*But he has gone. She stops, her back to* JACK.)

JACK: What was all that about? Lucy?

(*She doesn't move. Her back still to him.*)

LUCY: Jack. I've done something really stupid.

(*Then she turns and looks at him. A moment. Then—*)

JACK: (*Groan*) Oh, no. No. Don't tell me. I can guess.

LUCY: I went to his room. I didn't know what I was—Yes. Of course I knew what I was doing!

(*Yells of*—Jack! Jack—where are you!)

JACK: Bloody hell. Still, I suppose it's not incest.

LUCY: Feels like it, though. What'll I do?

(*Fractional pause. The cries, off, get nearer.*)

JACK: (*Sigh*) I could really have done with that cup of tea, you know.

(*She is suddenly enraged.*)

LUCY: Then lick it up!

(*He looks at her, then turns his head aside.*)

JACK: Yes. That's wholly appropriate. Yes. I'll do that.

(EDDIE *and* ELIZABETH *are coming through the side door, apparently arguing.*)

EDDIE: I'm telling you, there's no point. He's probably caught the ferry. We can't just wander around yelling our heads off.

ELIZABETH: There's no ferry on a Sunday. You know that.

EDDIE: There's not much else we can do in *this* heat. Lucy, we can't find—Jack!

(*Momentarily,* ELIZABETH *betrays her relief.*)

ELIZABETH: (*Rushing forward*) Jack—*there* you are!

JACK: And there *you* are.

(ELIZABETH *checks her movement toward him.*)

ELIZABETH: You stupid man! What are you trying to prove!

JACK: Elizabeth. You look ab–so–lute–ly ravishing. Doesn't she, Eddie? Hot but not bothered.

ELIZABETH: We've been all over the place looking for you!

EDDIE: Didn't you hear us?

JACK: Oh, I heard you. I heard you in my head. All night long.

ELIZABETH: Where *were* you? What were you doing?

JACK: Elizabeth. Would you make me a cup of tea, please?

ELIZABETH: Jack!

JACK: And then I want to talk to you, both of you. No, all of you. There are a few little things I want to clear up—

LUCY: That's right. So do I.

(*Little pause.*)

EDDIE: That seems to make sense.

ELIZABETH: I'd rather sit down and talk sensibly than have any more melodrama, Jack. We've got everything out of perspective—

JACK: Horizontal, and not vertical d'you mean?

EDDIE: What?

LUCY: Lying down instead of standing up.

ELIZABETH: If we're going to talk, let's do it properly. There's no need to snigger. We're not children, after all. We're all adult. Well—almost.

EDDIE: Where's Clayton?

LUCY: He—

JACK: (*Quickly*) He's gone down to the beach. I think he's being discreet.

LUCY: We—perhaps we ought to talk about Clayton too . . .

EDDIE: I don't want him involved in any more of this. The way you were sounding off, Lucy—just as though he wasn't there. I don't want him involved, OK? Keep him out of it. He's only a kid.

LUCY: He's not *blind*, Eddie . . .

EDDIE: Listen, the kid's not too stable, that's all. He gets into things too deep for his own good.

LUCY: (*Rueful*) You don't know how true that is!

EDDIE: What do you mean?

LUCY: You should have thought of Clayton last night. Asshole.

EDDIE: If we're going to talk, let's keep it cool. Otherwise, what's the point?

LUCY: Cool!

EDDIE: Either we've things to settle here, or we haven't. And we won't work anything out by calling each other names, that's for sure. (*Glares at* JACK.) Or by hitting and kicking—right?

(LUCY *suddenly breaks away*.)

Lucy—what are you doing?

LUCY: I'm going to look for Clayton.

EDDIE: What for?

(LUCY *stops. She stares at the trio.*)

58

JACK: He'll be all right. Lucy. He's OK. Leave him be for a while.

(EDDIE *looks from* LUCY *to* JACK.)

EDDIE: What's going on?

LUCY: We need a drink. If—if we're going to talk and—(*Severely*)—Elizabeth. Will you come with me, please?

(LUCY *does not wait for an answer, but turns away to the kitchen.* ELIZABETH *misunderstands, not knowing about the Lucy–Clayton business.*)

ELIZABETH: (*To* JACK) We're not living in the nineteenth century, are we? Why are you and Lucy taking it so—These things happen. You mustn't make mountains out of—out of—

JACK: Molehills.

ELIZABETH: No—I'm not saying it's trivial, what happened—but things like that have a history, Jack. They have reasons. And once you understand, you—and Lucy—you might not want to blow everything up and—

(*She trails off, silenced by the cold ferocity of* JACK*'s stare.*)

JACK: Lucy wants to talk to you.

ELIZABETH: No, she doesn't. She wants to claw my face with her fingernails.

EDDIE: No, no.

ELIZABETH: Oh, *yes*. I'm the Scarlet Woman.

JACK: Go and talk to her.

ELIZABETH: Why the hell should I?

EDDIE: (*Snarl*) Do as you're told!

(ELIZABETH *looks at* EDDIE, *in surprise. Then she turns away, sullen.*)

ELIZABETH: All right. It won't do any good. But work out which one of you is the Master, will you?

(ELIZABETH *goes to the kitchen, looking haughty.* EDDIE *watches her, then, trying to be nonchalant, or at least casual, sits on the recliner next to* JACK.)

EDDIE: Women.

JACK: Go on.

EDDIE: What?

JACK: 'God bless them.' You're supposed to add 'God bless them.' Or even 'What would we do without them?' (*Looks at*

EDDIE, *sadly*.)
In days of old when knights were bold
And women weren't invented
They carved holes in telegraph poles
And fucked till their heart's contented.
(EDDIE *laughs an awkward little laugh*.)

EDDIE: Keats again, I suppose.

JACK: (*Not smiling*) No. Shakespeare.
(*Awkward little pause*.)

EDDIE: I—ah—I think we all had too much to drink last night.

JACK: No. Too little.

EDDIE: I don't want to take Elizabeth away from you, Jack.

JACK: Ah. But you have. You already have.

EDDIE: Hell, no, Jack—it was just—no, it isn't like that, believe me.

JACK: Just one of those things, eh?

EDDIE: Well, in a way—No. Of course not. I wouldn't put it like that—but—

JACK: How would you put it?

EDDIE: Look—it was just something that happened, the way it does. There was sort of, a sort of chemistry, and—hell, you know what I mean.

JACK: Lust. You mean lust.

EDDIE: I don't think that's a very useful word, Jack. OK. I don't deny it's hell, yes, it's physical, of course it is, and—um—

JACK: Do you love her?
(EDDIE *puts his hand on* JACK, *would-be reassuring*.)

EDDIE: I never quite know what that means—

JACK: Kindly remove your paw.

EDDIE: Aw, now, Jack—

JACK: Remove it!
(EDDIE *does, and sighs*.)

EDDIE: Do you want to talk? Are you going to strike attitudes, or do you want to work things out? I've told you—I don't want to take her from you, and she doesn't want that either.
(*Little pause*.)

JACK: I hate your fucking guts.

EDDIE: Yes. I know that. But you always did, right?

JACK: Right!

EDDIE: (*Not without sympathy*) You poor slob.

> (JACK *turns his head away, suddenly overcome. He sucks in his breath, shudderingly, in a more or less vain effort to stop weeping.* EDDIE *looks at him, embarrassed.*)

> Don't, Jack. Please.

JACK: Christ. Oh, Christ.

EDDIE: Yeh. I know. I know.

> (*Pause.* JACK *controls himself.*)

JACK: I lay on the rocks last night and all I could see in the dark was your hands on her, your body on top of her, your mouth on her mouth, and—

> (*He stops.* EDDIE *looks down at his hands.*)

EDDIE: That's—listen, Jack—those are the wrong pictures—

JACK: And then I must have fallen asleep. Because suddenly it was light again, and I could see the ship.

EDDIE: What ship? Oh. The freighter—

JACK: It was coming clear out of the dawn. I felt as though I was on board, the deck trembling beneath my feet. I don't think there was ever before such a sight that filled me with such (*little pause*) absolute (*little pause*) grief.

> (*Pause.* EDDIE *stands up.*)

EDDIE: I'm sorry. I'm very sorry.

JACK: We're missing a trick in the food-processing business, you know.

EDDIE: Jack?

JACK: Instead of using dipotassium phosphate and sodium caseinate to replace milk in coffee and extra microbes to help *whippability* we ought to add blood and nerve tissue to our hamburgers. Human blood. Human tissue. Adequate protein. Sufficient carbohydrate.

EDDIE: What are you talking about?

JACK: People like to eat all sorts of things, Eddie, from snails to bullocks' testicles. But what they really want, what people really want to get between their teeth and slowly chew and swallow is other people. People want to eat people. They dribble at the mouth at the very thought of it. Have *you* got wet lips, Eddie? And blood on your teeth—eh?

EDDIE: Give it a rest, will you?

JACK: And what about my job? We mustn't forget that, must we? What about our dearly beloved Greenace, junk merchants to the masses?

(EDDIE *turns back, and looks at him.*)

EDDIE: You want to go into that? You really want to go into that?

JACK: Of course. I want to know where I stand. I don't necessarily need my self-respect, but I need my job. (*Sniff.*) The two things are incompatible, fortunately.

(EDDIE *measures him.*)

EDDIE: Jack. I've been in the business close on twenty years. And in all that time you are without doubt the most difficult, the most obstructive, the most inconsistent, the most argumentative, incompetent and disloyal pain in the ass I have ever encountered. And that's a fact.

JACK: You mean, I'm due for promotion.

(EDDIE *grins, half in exasperation.*)

EDDIE: Up, up and away, boy.

JACK: Level with me, as you people say.

EDDIE: (*Cutting in*) Who's 'you people'?

JACK: You bloody Americans, of course. You outa-my-way go-getting planet-polluters.

EDDIE: I see.

JACK: I doubt that, *old buddy*. I doubt whether you do.

EDDIE: Where does it come from? All that bile in you. That hate. Did your mother never bake you apple pie?

(JACK *looks at him, then his eyes slide away.*)

JACK: They want to get rid of me, don't they? I'm for the high jump. I'm going to be kicked out. They'll find a way. Contract or no contract. Shares or no shares.

EDDIE: Not necessarily. And not if I can help it.

(JACK *looks back at him again, suspicious.*)

JACK: What do you mean?

EDDIE: This vacation, Jack. It was kind of my idea.

JACK: Why? So that you could sleep with my wife?

(EDDIE *spreads his hands.*)

62

EDDIE: OK. OK. So you don't want to listen.

JACK: All right. What was the *other* purpose? Come on. I want to know.

EDDIE: Well, that's all shot to pieces now. But I wanted us to get away from the offices and—I wanted to try to make you see once and for all that there's no percentage in being deliberately obstructive toward policies already determined, strategies already under way. I was hoping we could use this space to put our heads together on this biotech business. For instance, it's a fact that mushrooms reproduce unstably, so you get them in different sizes. You've been concentrating on the picking end, but we want to crack the problem of the way they reproduce. Their genetics. We've got to live with this biotech business, Jack. Believe me.

JACK: When it comes to bacterial protein, old son, I'd rather eat humble pie.

EDDIE: Then that's what you'll have to chew, Jack. I promise you.

JACK: Are you threatening me?

(*Little pause.*)

EDDIE: Let's go into this some other time, Jack. There's too much between us at the moment. Neither of us is in a position to be rational. We'll—(*Suddenly*) Wake yourself up, man! Stop wallowing in your own sense of disillusion and disappointment! Do you think the things that happen to you happen by *chance*? Take a good look at Elizabeth—why would she tumble in the hay with *me*? For Christ's sake, a blind man can see she loves you.

(*Pause.*)

JACK: Piss off, will you.

EDDIE: Ach! I'd like to shake the shit out of you.

JACK: Come on, then. Try. Just try it, big mouth.

(JACK *hauls himself up, belligerent.*)

EDDIE: Oh sit down, you idiot.

JACK: Come on. Come on. Let's see what you can do. Big mouth.

EDDIE: You might use your fists on a woman, but you won't be able to use them on *me*.

JACK: We'll see about that!

(JACK *squares up to a contemptuously indifferent* EDDIE*: but, comically, even touchingly,* JACK *holds his fists in the antique bare-knuckle prize-fighter stance, as in an old sporting print.*)

EDDIE: What the hell are you doing?

JACK: Put 'em up! Put 'em up!

(*Comically, in his antique stance,* JACK *circles round* EDDIE*, flashing out a threatening left, but nowhere near connecting.*)

EDDIE: Jack! Are you crazy!

(*A rather tentative left fist lands on* EDDIE*'s shoulder.*)

JACK: I'm going to give you a bloody good hiding—!

(JACK *dances threateningly around* EDDIE*, who has not put his fists up. And, again without much conviction,* JACK *lands another blow.*)

EDDIE: Jack—stop it—now stop it! I don't want to hurt you—!

(*And* JACK *hits him, harder.* EDDIE*, exasperated, pushes* JACK *in the face with the palm of his open hand. Caught off balance, and in poor condition,* JACK *staggers back helplessly, tries to right himself, fails, and bumps down hard on his backside, a look of comical astonishment on his face. At the exact moment that* LUCY *and* ELIZABETH *come back from their talk in the kitchen.* LUCY *is carrying a tray of cups. The women are astounded.*)

ELIZABETH: Eddie—!

EDDIE: (*Quickly*) I didn't hit him. I only pushed. I had to!

LUCY: He's in no condition, Eddie!

EDDIE: I didn't hit him. I didn't!

JACK: (*On ground*) Rot in hell! You bastard!

ELIZABETH: Jack. Stop it!

LUCY: Eddie—this is stupid.

EDDIE: This is none of my doing. He's trying to knock me down. What am I supposed to do? (*To* JACK*, hand outstretched*) Come on, Jack. Get up. Don't be ridiculous.

JACK: I don't need *your* help, thank you very much.

(*He half rises, but then, exhausted, falls back again.*)

ELIZABETH: For goodness' sake. You look so ludicrous. Jack—do you know what you look like?

JACK: I don't want to get up, do I? I'm going to stay here. I'm perfectly content to stay here. Sod it. Sod all of you.

ELIZABETH: Do you want your cup of tea?

JACK: Tea? Have you made tea?

LUCY: (*Irritated*) Let's go inside. Into the shade. We'll be barbecued out here.

(EDDIE *wipes his brow*.)

EDDIE: It must be well over a hundred. I don't know why I picked this place. It's the pits.

(*As they move into the living room*—)

ELIZABETH: (*To* JACK, *as she goes in*) You'll roast there. Get up, and don't be such a fool! Jack!

JACK: Leave me alone. Cow.

(LUCY *puts the tray on to the table in the living room.* EDDIE, LUCY *and then* ELIZABETH *take their tea*.)

EDDIE: I wish we could all go home this minute. I wish we could leave this place—Why don't we? Now *there*'s an idea . . .

LUCY: Eddie. We're worried about Clayton.

EDDIE: How do you mean?

(JACK, *still on his backside on the terrace, seems suddenly alert, listening*.)

LUCY: (*Evasive*) He—well, he's in a state about everything here. He *really* wants to leave, I think.

ELIZABETH: (*Looking at* JACK) And Lucy doesn't know where he's gone.

(*The two women have obviously talked about it*.)

EDDIE: But he's always off on his own. Swimming. Walking. Anything. But, sure, let's *all* get the hell out.

LUCY: He was—very upset.

EDDIE: You shouldn't talk in front of him like you did. That was all wrong. Is he worried about it? Did he *say*?

LUCY: He—Oh, Christ—

ELIZABETH: It's something else, Eddie.

(*Little pause.* EDDIE *looks at* LUCY. JACK, *on the terrace, gets up*.)

EDDIE: What's happened? What are you talking about?

(JACK *quietly goes off the terrace by the side steps, and not through the living room*.)

LUCY: I don't think I can tell you.

EDDIE: Elizabeth—what's going on!

LUCY: (*Suddenly*) I went to Clayton's room last night.

EDDIE: You what?

ELIZABETH: She didn't know what to do, Eddie. She was out of her mind.

EDDIE: (*Incredulous*) But—but—you're not saying you—Lucy? You *didn't*? Did you?

(ELIZABETH *and* LUCY *look at each other*.)

LUCY: Yes.

EDDIE: You—you bitch! You—Lucy! You couldn't! You didn't!

LUCY: I was—I felt hurt. Physically. Emotionally. I—

(*Her voice threatens to break*.)

EDDIE: What's that to do with it! Why'd you have to involve *him*! He's not playing games. He's too vulnerable! For Christ's sake, Lucy! You're—you're *disgusting*—! That's practically *incest*.

ELIZABETH: Don't. Eddie. Stop it. And it isn't anyway—

EDDIE: Keep out of it, you!

ELIZABETH: Don't be such a bully! What's good enough for the goose is good enough for the gosling.

EDDIE: Lucy. I'll never forgive you for this. Never.

LUCY: (*Scream*) And do you think I'll ever forgive *you*—!

ELIZABETH: What a mess. Reminds me of Christmas when I was a child.

EDDIE: Smart ass.

LUCY: You two were in my bed—Jack had gone crazy—I—I listened outside your door, and—

ELIZABETH: Oh, God. Say no more. This is worse than *The Archers*.

LUCY: I went to *your* room, Elizabeth. My—(*Controls herself*.) My eye was throbbing. I couldn't think. I just wanted to lie down and pull the covers over my head. But—I couldn't stay in that room. There was—there was your perfume or —something on the pillow. And Jack might come in and—I couldn't stay there I—I just couldn't—No way . . .

(*She begins to cry quietly*. ELIZABETH *suddenly embraces her*. EDDIE, *stiff, cold, stands off*.)

ELIZABETH: Of course you couldn't, Lucy. Of course you couldn't.

(LUCY *again controls herself*.)

LUCY: I wanted somebody to—just to put a pair of arms around me—I've never felt so—(*Her voice hardens, and she looks at* EDDIE.) And so I went to Clayton. Why not?

EDDIE: But what about *him*? Did you care a dime about *him*?

LUCY: I don't know how it happened. I don't—he—it sort of— He took over. It was as near to rape as—No. That's not fair. But once I was in there, I couldn't—I got out as soon as I could.

EDDIE: But did he—I mean—did you actually—you know. . . ?

LUCY: No.

(*Little pause.* EDDIE *expels his breath.*)

EDDIE: You mean—nothing really happened—?

LUCY: (*Yell*) No!

(ELIZABETH *looks at her in bewilderment.*)

ELIZABETH: But I thought you said—(*She checks herself.*) Yes. Right. You're right.

EDDIE: I don't get this—

ELIZABETH: (*Cutting in*) It was the same with us. Wasn't it? Eddie? Nothing happened.

(*But* EDDIE *is concerned about Clayton.*)

EDDIE: Where has he gone? Lucy—what did you say to him after we left? You got to tell me.

LUCY: He—he imagines he's in love with me.

EDDIE: What?

ELIZABETH: Well—he would, wouldn't he? A boy like that.

EDDIE: In *love* with you? What a lot of shit! What you going to do about it? Send him a valentine card?

LUCY: You're a thug, Eddie. In so many ways. You—no wonder Clayton can't talk with you. The first thing we need to do is to find him, and then—let me sort it out. Let me talk to him. On my own.

EDDIE: I'm not handing him over to you! You're not going to get *near* him, understand? You've done enough damage— (*He breaks off, seeing their faces—They can see* JACK *returning with* CLAYTON, *on to the terrace.* EDDIE *turns, then plunges forward—*) Clayton!

(*But as he reaches out, the youth recoils.*)

JACK: Leave it, Eddie!

(EDDIE *checks his stride.*)

67

EDDIE: Are you OK, son?

CLAYTON: Leave me alone.

EDDIE: But—sure. OK. But—if you want to talk—with me, just
with me—

CLAYTON: What about?

EDDIE: Well—last night or—well, anything—
(CLAYTON *looks at him, then wordless, strides off, toward the stairs.*
LUCY *has little chance to intercept.*)

LUCY: Clayton—
(*He does not stop, nor look at her. But half-way up the stairs, he
turns and looks down.*)

CLAYTON: I'm going to pack my bag. I'm getting out of this
place. It needs fumigating.

LUCY: Clayton—
(*He turns away. Then stops, looks back.*)

CLAYTON: All right. I know you're laughing at me. I know it's
funny.

LUCY: I'm not, Clayton. I'm not. Of course I'm not—
(*But he turns, abrupt, and strides on up the stair. Little pause.*
JACK, *apparently unconcerned, picks up a cup.*)

JACK: Do you realize how long I've had to wait for this? (*He
drinks.*) Yuk! It's *coffee*. And it's *cold*.

ELIZABETH: Where was he, Jack?

JACK: It's also got *sugar* in it.

EDDIE: He can't leave like this. There are no flights out until
Wednesday anyway.

ELIZABETH: Worse luck.

JACK: O for a beaker of the cold North. A steaming mug of thick
brown tea. Eh? Wouldn't that be nice? (*No change of tone.*)
Go up and talk to him, Lucy. Put your arms around him.

LUCY: Oh, but—

JACK: No—go on. Talk to him. *Please.*

EDDIE: Oh no you don't. *I* will.

JACK: What? And kiss his tears away? You must be joking! He
wants the bandage, not the wound. Lucy hasn't really done
him any harm. He'll just see her face floating in the stars
for a while, but—(*shrug*)—then he'll start to masturbate, for
the sake of auld lang syne.

68

EDDIE: We're talking about *my son* here.

JACK: Ah, yes. But Clayton doesn't know how to—what is it you people say?—*communicate*. Clayton doesn't know how to communicate with you, Eddie. Not yet he doesn't. If you go up to him now, he'll simply stare at the wall and then at the floor until the words dry up in your throat. (*Little pause.*) You must have noticed the same thing at the office.

EDDIE: Ach!

LUCY: But Clayton won't want *me* there, Jack—

JACK: At the moment he's not sure whether he's Romeo or Oedipus, Casanova or the Hunchback of Notre-Dame. A bit of each, I should imagine. Lucky sod. Lucy, my sweet, I wish to Christ someone like you had come quietly into *my* bed when I was his age. It would have saved me an awful lot of bother. (*Looks at* ELIZABETH.) And a great deal of stupid romanticism.

EDDIE: We're talking about *my son* and *my wife*—

JACK: I'm sure we're all grateful for your constant reminders of who is related to whom. Any moment now you'll discover what is related to what.

EDDIE: What happened, happened. It shouldn't have involved Clayton.

LUCY: Did he say anything to you, Jack? What was he doing?

JACK: He was sitting in a cave down by the shore. Cross-legged. And rocking to and fro, banging his back against the rock at the narrow end of the cave.

EDDIE: He was *what*? I don't believe you—

ELIZABETH: How did you know where to look?

JACK: Because I've sat there myself, my soiled love. Cross-legged. Not exactly rocking to and fro, and certainly not banging my back against the rock. It was my head actually. Makes a change from hitting it against a brick wall. So—I knew exactly where a wounded animal would go to lick its sensibilities.

EDDIE: Oh, play the violins.

ELIZABETH: (*Reaching out*) Jack—

JACK: (*Abrupt*) Tuesday afternoons and Thursday mornings.
  (EDDIE *and* ELIZABETH *look at each other.* LUCY *notices.*)

LUCY: Is—is that when—?

JACK: That's right. That's when your husband screwed my wife. In my bed. As regular as clockwork. Tick tock. Or rather, knowing the bed in question, *creak creak*.

EDDIE: It wasn't like—it's not the way you put it—

JACK: Unless, that is, they merely met for coffee and seed cake. Or tea and sympathy. I shouldn't have thought there was sufficient carbohydrate in either, would you, Eddie?

LUCY: (*Flat*) I knew it. I knew.

(*Little pause.* ELIZABETH *goes to speak, then stops herself.*)

JACK: You *read* much, Eddie? Any bestsellers? Things like that?

EDDIE: What?

JACK: Do you go to the theatre? Or the cinema? Be bop a loo bop. Eh?

EDDIE: What are you talking about. . . ?

JACK: Because I've been wondering where the hell you got the idea that adultery is a little piece of adult behaviour that doesn't matter very much any more. It's just an entertainment, right? Something up there in lights to make us snigger and chortle, all we sophisticates. Don't you know the endless—endless—ache of it—?

ELIZABETH: Jack. Listen—

(*But he ignores her, and keeps his attention clamped on* EDDIE.)

JACK: Or maybe it's something you picked up at work, is it, Eddie? A bit of seasoning salt to add to the diet, sprinkled on what we otherwise couldn't swallow. Things difficult to digest like—love and duty and commitment and—

EDDIE: You say your father was a preacher?

JACK: Shut your dirty mouth.

(*Pause.* EDDIE *twitches a little.*)

ELIZABETH: (*Carefully*) You think you had nothing to do with any of this, Jack? You're not responsible for it in any way at all? I've never done anything like this before. No matter what you think. Can you accept that some of it might be your own fault? Jack?

(JACK *looks at her, then*—)

JACK: Aren't we going to get anything to eat today?

ELIZABETH: You see! You see!

70

LUCY: (*Deliberately*) You want me to cook something, Jack?

JACK: I could eat a horse, Lucy. Preferably Pegasus.

LUCY: And I could eat *ashes*.

JACK: Sorry. I don't think there's anything from the Greenace range in the larder. It's mostly natural, unprocessed stuff, I'm afraid. Wholesome things, and unprofitable muck like that. Why don't you stay hungry and go see to Clayton.

EDDIE: No!

LUCY: (*Ignoring* EDDIE) You think I should, Jack? I don't know what to say to him—except sorry. And he won't like that.

EDDIE: Don't say anything. Just keep away from him.

LUCY: (*Again pointedly ignoring* EDDIE) What do you think, Jack?

EDDIE: Lucy—

JACK: (*Cutting in*) All you have to do is remember what it was like to be *his* age, Lucy. Half of you, then, at least half of you, is still the child for whom the world and everything in it is filled to the brim with fear and wonder. Or both, mixed up together. None of your fast-fading violets covered up with leaves. None of our elaborate yawns. Everything— when it's not dangerous, and even when it is—everything is still new enough to—sort of glisten from inside. To shimmer in your mind. Don't you remember? Jesus, I do! And I'll bet Clayton still knows it. I'm sure he does.

EDDIE: Not now he doesn't!

(JACK *looks at him, and, suddenly smiles from ear to ear.*)

JACK: How extraordinary.

EDDIE: What's so funny?

JACK: How very extraordinary.

ELIZABETH: Jack?

JACK: Talking about Clayton—I suddenly—(*Turns to* EDDIE, *delighted.*) I thought my ability to decide *anything* had totally atrophied, along with my red corpuscles. Eddie. I've got good news for you. Really splendid news. I am not going back to Greenace. Not even to clear my desk.

ELIZABETH: (*Quickly*) Don't be hasty, Jack.

JACK: I'm not going back! I'm not going back!

EDDIE: OK. If that's what you want.

JACK: New enough and bright enough and—(*Almost a little jig.*)

71

How extraordinary! How bloody extraordinary!

EDDIE: I think you're making a wise decision. You've never been happy with us. I suggest you stay right here on this island, and talk to the birds. But don't get offended when they shit on you—they don't mean it.

LUCY: Don't talk to him like that!

EDDIE: (*Shrug*) How do you talk to someone who's nuts?

(JACK *laughs with delight.* LUCY *smiles.*)

ELIZABETH: But Eddie! He's got nowhere else to go! Nobody else would put up with him! I didn't mean it quite like that, Jack. I meant—

JACK: (*Delighted*) Quite right, Liz! Quite right! You've hit the nail on the head. No—*into* my head! It's time I put up with *myself*—(*He stops.*) Did you hear that? Did you hear the ship's hooter? Out in the bay.

LUCY: No.

JACK: Listen!

(*Small pause.* JACK *is no longer smiling, but seems curiously tense.*)

EDDIE: I should watch it, Jack. Now you're starting to hear things.

(JACK, *his mood apparently swiftly changed, looks at* EDDIE.)

JACK: (*Quietly*) I wouldn't be surprised. I wouldn't be a bit surprised.

(*Abruptly, and seemingly as swiftly morose as he was cheerful,* JACK *walks away, back out on to the terrace, to take up the same position as he was at the beginning of the play. Looking intently out to sea. They watch him, puzzled.* EDDIE *shrugs. Then—*)

ELIZABETH: You mustn't listen to him, Eddie. He's obviously not himself. He can't think straight. His job's important to him, I know that. And I'm damned sure it's important to *me*.

(LUCY's *attention has been fixed on* JACK *for some time. She seems to be expecting something of him, and is not listening to the other two.*)

LUCY: (*To no one*) What is he doing out there? What's he looking for?

EDDIE: (*To* ELIZABETH) I can't work with him. Not after all this. I never *could* come to that. He's all piss and vinegar, and I honestly think you should make him see a doctor.

ELIZABETH: Oh, come on.

EDDIE: No. I mean it. He's on the edge, Elizabeth, the very edge.
I've seen it before with others.

LUCY: (*Not listening*) What's he looking at?

EDDIE: Who knows? Christ walking on the water, maybe.

ELIZABETH: Eddie! Stop it!

(JACK *has raised his hand to his eyes, the better to peer out over the
sea, like an old mariner looking for land. Then—*)

JACK: (*Calls*) Come and see!

(*They don't move. Then* LUCY *takes a step forward, but hesitates,
and stops.*)

EDDIE: It's too hot out there. The sun's right overhead now.
He'll sizzle his eyeballs. It's already burnt out his brains.

JACK: Come and look at this! Quickly! Lucy—Elizabeth
—Eddie—look!

(*Half curious, half reluctant, they troop out on to the terrace.*)

LUCY: What is it?

ELIZABETH: What are you looking at?

JACK: The ship. Look. The old black freighter. The one I was
telling you about.

(*There is no excitement, no exuberance in his voice: but a sort of
restrained awe with a suggestion of amusement. The others peer into
the distance. As they do,* CLAYTON *appears on the stairs behind
them, with a shoulder bag. He hesitates. Stops. Listens.*)

LUCY: Where, Jack?

ELIZABETH: I can't see anything—

(*She looks suspiciously, even fearfully, at* JACK.)

JACK: Over there. Where the—there. Where the sky and the sea
come together.

EDDIE: (*Abrupt*) There's nothing there.

LUCY: Are you sure, Jack?

(*On the stairs,* CLAYTON *drops his bag. He seems interested.*)

JACK: Oh, it's not much more than a tiny smudge. You have to
know precisely where to look, and exactly what you're
looking for. See—right there! Right on the edge of the
world. (*Laughs, then stops.*) If you squeeze your eyelids
together you can just about make it out. Crawling along on
top of the sea between the blue and the blue. God, isn't that
light amazing? Have you ever experienced anything so

73

totally, absolutely *lucid*.

EDDIE: That's more than can be said of you, Jack. There's no
ship out there. You're making it up—or imagining things.

JACK: (*Tenderly, softly*) Poor little ship. Poor brave lost little
vessel. But it keeps on. It keeps going.

EDDIE: There's nothing there. Nothing *I* want.

(EDDIE *turns away, contemptuously. And stops. He has seen*
CLAYTON. *Father and son look at each other.*)

ELIZABETH: What are you talking about, Jack? What are you
playing at? (*Suspiciously*) Are you feeling all right?

LUCY: I'd like to see it. I wish I could see it.

(JACK'*s eyes have not moved off the horizon. He smiles to himself.*)

JACK: You've got to use your eyes properly. It's there. Oh, it's
there all right. It's been there all the time. You just have to
remember what it looks like.

(LUCY *looks at him, puzzled.* ELIZABETH *looks at him,*
apprehensive.)

EDDIE: Clayton?

(CLAYTON *does not respond.* LUCY *and* ELIZABETH *turn.* JACK *does*
not move, but he seems deliberately to raise the pitch of his voice.)

JACK: When I was a lad I used to dream of being an old tramp
steamer like that one out there. Taking ingots and cast iron
and *ordinary* baubles, *usual* beads. And coming home with
cinnamon and coriander and silks and—the world was
waiting, full of so many sunlit harbours and snow-capped
mountains. Sometimes the deck would be awash with huge
waves, but often the ocean was as smooth and calm as the
mirror I scarcely ever dared gaze at too closely. But in the
water, I could see my own—My own soul. My own cargo.
My own ship.

(*He stops.* CLAYTON *comes on down the stairs, eyes on* JACK, *and on*
to the terrace.)

EDDIE: You OK, son?

JACK: (*Not turning*) It took me a long, long time to realize that I
actually *was* on a journey. Even just sitting there, or lying
awake, anywhere, everywhere, no matter what, I was on a
journey. And then, when I understood this, I went and
forgot it. Somehow or other I lost the sense of it. Lost my

74

compass. That's why I'm glad I can see that battered old boat out there, trundling along from one end of time to the other.

(CLAYTON *stands right next to* JACK.)

CLAYTON: (*Earnest*) Where? Where is it, Jack?

(JACK *stiffens a little, then points.*)

JACK: Way out there. I don't know whether you can see it.

(CLAYTON *looks, intently. Silence. Then he looks at* JACK, *and says nothing.* EDDIE *feels vaguely jealous.*)

EDDIE: You're crazy! You're starting to see things that aren't even there. You can't see it, can you, Clayton? What's so special about an old boat anyway?

JACK: If we were on board, rolling a bit as we braced our feet on the deck, we'd have a stronger sense of being on the journey. Like now. Right now. It's a bit stormy, and a bit misty. Eh, Clayton?

(*For the first time,* JACK *looks at the boy.* CLAYTON *hesitates, then nods.*)

CLAYTON: Yeh. Very.

(JACK *smiles, and again looks out to sea.*)

ELIZABETH: (*Irritated*) It's clear out there. Clear as a bell.

JACK: (*Ignoring her*) Well, that's what it's like on a voyage, old son. *The* voyage. We don't necessarily know exactly where we are going. Mind you, it would be a pity if we did, because then we'd never be surprised by unexpected islands or the visiting albatross. Look at that old boat! I think they're all up on deck. There's not much point in staying down below in the hold. That's like sitting in a cave. Christ—we know what's down there—the stuff we brought with us, the lumber. Got a bad smell. It doesn't always keep, does it?

(*Little pause.*)

CLAYTON: No. It doesn't.

(*Almost absent-mindedly, it seems,* JACK *lets his hand rest on* CLAYTON's *shoulder.*)

JACK: It only came back to me a little while ago. The image of myself with my head in my hands, cowering in the bowels of the black freighter. Seeing nothing new with a fresh eye.

75

Things make you want to do that sometimes. You feel you
have to hide.

CLAYTON: Yeh.

EDDIE: (*Irritated*) What are you talking about? Are you some kind
of ostrich?

CLAYTON: Yeh.

(JACK *smiles*, LUCY *laughs*.)

JACK: Trouble is, the ship is still rolling, the timbers are still
creaking, the foam is still washing behind it, measuring
where we've been. We're on it, like it or not. But you have
to get back on deck, and brace yourself, before you can see
where you are. You can get some idea by the smell of the
wind or the position of the stars. They're the sound of other
people's voices. People who are on a voyage too. They kind
of feel lost at times, Clayton. We can't help it. It's the
nature of the vessel, old son. And the peril of the journey.
But—you're not *starting* from here, you're already on the
way.

(*Pause.* CLAYTON *looks at him.*)

CLAYTON: It's a mess though. A real mess.

JACK: We don't get time to look at the shape of our lives, the
chart of our transit. Or, rather, we *do* get time, plenty of
time, but we don't care to use it. That's why I'm glad to be
able to see that old freighter out there. (*Laughs suddenly, and
calls—with glee*) *Ahoy there!* You cunning old bugger!

(*Little pause. Then* CLAYTON *laughs.*)

ELIZABETH: (*Suddenly*) I'm not going away, Jack. I don't want
you to twist things out of—

(*She stops. He doesn't look at her, but stiffens.* JACK *then turns to
them, almost mockingly.*)

JACK: Don't tell me you can't see it. Take another look. Go on!

(*Little pause. They look again.*)

EDDIE: There's no ship out there. And you're nuts, Jack. Really
nuts.

ELIZABETH: I—no. I can't see anything. Jack—

(*Pause.*)

LUCY: (*Wry, affectionate*) Mmm. Maybe. I'm not sure. I—no,
Jack. Not quite.

(*Pause.*)

CLAYTON: (*Flat*) Yes. I can see it.

JACK: (*Softly*) That's right, Clayton. I knew you could. Your eyes are tuned to it.

CLAYTON: It's kind of—kind of like—looking into glass—

JACK: A reflecting glass. No. (*Laughs.*) Through a glass darkly.

CLAYTON: Sure. Yes. (*Starts to laugh.*) I can see it! I can! You're right, Jack! It's there, OK!

(*Pause.* EDDIE, LUCY, ELIZABETH *look at* CLAYTON, *puzzled. Then, suddenly,* CLAYTON *puts his hands up to his face, defensively, and starts to weep.* EDDIE *frowns, moves to him.*)

EDDIE: There's no need to—listen to me, Clay . . .

LUCY: (*Quickly, loudly*) Oh, yes! I've got it now! I see it, Jack! I can see it!

ELIZABETH: Where? Where?

(CLAYTON's *swift tears turn to strained laughter.*)

LUCY: (*With desperate insistence*) I see it!

(ELIZABETH *takes her cue, at last.*)

ELIZABETH: Oh. Yes. Of course. Yes! There it is!

(*The light is fading, fast.*)

EDDIE: (*Irritated*) Why are you falling for this crap? You've got eyes. You've got brains. Use them! There's no ship out there. Just a floating pulpit. A fucking pulpit! What are you playing at, Jack? How many angels are dancing on the head of *your* pin?

(CLAYTON, JACK, LUCY, ELIZABETH *begin to laugh.*)

Yeh! It *is* funny. Damn it to hell. It's crazy!

(*They stop laughing. They hold still. Blackout. Sound in the dark, of ship's hooter, long and plangent. The light gradually comes up again to reveal* JACK *and* CLAYTON, *alone, as they were in Act One.*)

JACK: When it passes, the ship, the light is even more opaque than it is now. Sort of—marbled. And cool. There are a few wisps of mist curling about an inch from the top of the sea, and yet the water is still that impossible blue—It's all like when the world began, and God Saw That It Was Good—(*Bitter little laugh.*) A chalice full of the warm South. The sea slap—slapping itself. The little olive trees catching hold of the rocks. Space. Air. And an uncertain smudge which sort

of—*solidifies* out of the ache in the mind and very
slowly becomes a black freighter dragging itself across the
edge of the world—For a moment—a whole minute—it's all
so perfect you want to reach out and—and pull it into your
soul. You want to pick it all up—and *eat it*. (*He turns.*) Do
you understand?

(*There is an intensity in the question which troubles the boy, who
responds with a strained laugh—the kind that is bound to leave him
stranded if* JACK *did not respond.*)

CLAYTON: That would be one heck of a mouthful.

(JACK *stares at him.* CLAYTON *wilts. Then* JACK *starts to laugh.*
CLAYTON, *relieved, smiles. They look at each other a long moment.
And then, in a sudden, compulsive, fragile humanity, the two
embrace. Light fades out.*)